MW00479498

STROKE OF Death

A Scarlet Cove SEASIDE COZY MYSTERY

Agatha Frost
& Evelyn Amber

pink tree
PUBLISHING

First published in print January 31st 2018

All characters and events in this publication, other than those clearly in the public domain, are fictitious and any resemblance to real persons, living or dead, is purely coincidental.

For questions and comments about this book, please contact
pinktreepublishing@gmail.com

www.pinktreepublishing.com
www.agathafrost.com
www.evelynamber.com

Edited by Keri Lierman and Karen Sellers

ISBN: 9781977041326
Imprint: Independently published

ALSO BY AGATHA FROST & EVELYN AMBER

The Scarlet Cove Series

Dead in the Water

Castle on the Hill

Stroke of Death

ALSO BY AGATHA FROST

The Peridale Café Series

Pancakes and Corpses

Lemonade and Lies

Doughnuts and Deception

Chocolate Cake and Chaos

Shortbread and Sorrow

Espresso and Evil

Macarons and Mayhem

Fruit Cake and Fear

Birthday Cake and Bodies

Gingerbread and Ghosts

A

Scarlet Cove

SEASIDE COZY MYSTERY

Book Three

One

Liz Jones looked down at the oddly shaped cookie dough on the baking tray. She had been aiming for perfect circles, but they looked more like beige chicken nuggets.

"I followed the instructions on the box," she said to her best friend, Nancy Turtle, as they both stared at the mess. "I *knew* I should have bought some from the corner shop. I *can't* bake."

"They're abstract," Nancy said with a firm nod,

her head tilting. "I bet they'll taste nice. Isn't that the whole point of buying the ingredients in a box? You can't go wrong with it."

"And yet here we are," Liz said as she crammed the tray into the pre-heated oven. "Let's cross our fingers."

Liz scratched at her frizzy red hair as she read the baking instructions on the side of the box. Had she even set the right temperature? The previous tenant had scrubbed off the markings around the dial, leaving her clueless.

It had been six months since she had moved to Scarlet Cove to make a fresh start. She had craved a slower pace of life after fifteen years in the police force, and that was what she had found. She painted more than ever, had made real friends, and had even adopted a dog, giving her a daily excuse to walk around the picturesque fishing town.

Liz had hoped the slower pace of life would have instilled some of the homemaking skills in her that she had always lacked; it had not. She could solve a murder case like nobody else, and yet she could not bake a simple tray of biscuits.

"I'm going to leave the baking to the

professionals," Liz said, tossing the box into the bin, where her microwave meal boxes also lay. "Let's go down to the shop. I heard some more people arrive."

Leaving the cookies in the oven, they headed to the front door, Liz's adopted beagle, Paddy, hot on their heels. Leaving the warmth of her flat, they walked next door to Liz's shop, '*Blank Canvas*'. Most of her recently formed art group had already arrived for their evening session.

"Great turnout," Nancy said as she pushed open the door. "I must say this was one of my better ideas."

Liz had to agree. She had moved to the coast to revel in the stunning views and paint them at her leisure. Nancy, who was a receptionist at the local art gallery, had suggested they set up a club for other people to join her. It had surprised Liz that she had not come up with the idea herself because of the natural fit. According to Nancy, people often inquired at the gallery about art classes. The gallery's suffocating manager, Katelyn Monroe, thought classes were '*common*'.

"I've told you before, Picasso is *wildly* overrated," announced Catherine Ford, the oldest member of the group, at sixty-one. "There's so much mysticism behind his art, but you know he only died in 1973. Hardly one of the *great* classics."

"*How* can you say that?" exclaimed Debbie Wood, the thick and plentiful bangles on each wrist jingling as she tossed her hands up. "He was a *genius* with colour and shape! His art is *transcendent*!"

"I never did care for all that abstract nonsense myself," added Trevor Swan, the wealthy, stocky owner of the Scarlet Cove Manor Hotel. "I much prefer a nice landscape."

"Anyone can paint a landscape," Debbie said, visibly exhausted by the reluctance of her fellow members. "I can't believe what I'm hearing!"

"Isn't that the beauty of art?" Liz called out, her smile wide, eager to defuse the tension before it grew out of hand. "There are *no* rules to follow, so we break them every time we pick up a brush. Everyone can have an opinion, but it doesn't mean they're right, does it?"

The trio considered Liz's words for a moment, glancing at each other out of the corner of their eyes.

"I *still* don't like Picasso," Catherine announced as she stared at Debbie over her glasses. "It gives me a headache trying to understand it."

"But that's what makes *great* art!" Debbie cried with a disbelieving laugh. "Art to make you think."

Liz concealed a smile as the trio disbanded; they were never going to come to a solid conclusion. Since starting her group, she had grown to like Debbie, who was as unconventional as people came. She always wore floor-length skirts with off-the-shoulder tunics, both usually paint-splattered. She had bangles stacked from wrists to forearms, and chunky rings on every finger. There was always a gold pendant wrapped around her bushy hair to rest on her forehead.

It did not take Liz's detective skills to see why Catherine and Debbie rarely saw eye to eye when it came to art. Whereas Debbie used every crayon in the box when it came to her wardrobe, Catherine only used one; grey. Her neatly trimmed hair was always blow-dried off her sharp, bird-like face. She always wore a plain and professional grey or black trouser suit and had her glasses chained around her neck for convenience. She reminded Liz of a librarian without any of the warmth and charm.

Debbie had an abstract style, whereas Catherine painted delicate watercolours of the seaside. Liz appreciated both of their styles, but she could not imagine them hanging on a wall next to each other.

While the group set up their easels, Liz arranged fruit in a copper bowl she had found in one of the town's many charity shops. She had always thought fruit was a good test of an artist's interpretation skills. It was such a basic and simple set-up, and yet with the right eye, it could transform into something magical.

"Sorry I'm late!" announced Lance Bennett as he burst through the door, his easel strung over his back. "I had to walk. Couldn't get my car past a herd of sheep on the top road."

Lance dumped his things in his usual spot in front of the window. He was the most skilled artist, and judging by his worldly appearance, the most travelled of the group. Whatever the assignment, he rose to it and demonstrated his mastery of many styles. Liz would have sworn a dozen different people had painted his collection of work.

After assembling his stool, he pulled the tie out of his sun-kissed hair, letting it fall over his face. He ran his fingers through it before securing it on top of his head in a messy bun. Not only was he a skilled artist, he was also handsome, especially for a man nearing his forties, not that he was Liz's type. She was happy with her farmer boyfriend, Simon Greene, but she could appreciate Lance's beauty. She often noticed the women of the group glancing at him when he was in his painter's world.

Polly Spragg, the ditzy hairdresser, and her grandmother, Sylvia Spragg, completed the circle. Liz flicked on the radio for background noise before setting up her own space in the group. She selected her acrylic paints from her collection before sketching out her composition.

Liz had set up the group as a class of sorts, but she rarely taught anything. She offered opinions on style and concept when asked, but that was as far as it went. When she caught Nancy's eyes, she remembered that her friend was an exception to that rule.

"It doesn't look right," Nancy whispered to Liz when she wandered over to see what she had done so far. "It looks childish."

Nancy, by her own admission, was not a skilled artist, despite being a great admirer of art. She had joined the group to absorb the surrounding talent, but she had yet to improve. Liz looked at the literal drawing of the fruit, wondering how to kindly frame her criticism.

"Composition is key," Liz said as she glanced at Lance's graffiti interpretation. "You're looking and seeing a bunch of bananas, apples, and oranges, but you should see shapes and colours. Zoom in and see beyond what is in front of you. Think about how the light hits the shapes, and go from there."

Nancy wiggled her glasses, scrunching up her nose as she stared deeper at the fruit. After a moment of observation, she decided a stalk on the apple was the missing element. Liz gave Nancy's shoulder a reassuring squeeze, but she knew it was going to take more than that to teach her the basics.

"I *think* I understand what you're talking about," Nancy said as she tapped her pencil on her chin. "I'll be fine."

Nancy gulped hard before grabbing the brightest shade of yellow in the box. Liz almost advised her to work up to that colour, but Nancy squirted it onto her palette with gusto. Liz decided to let her discover her artistic eye in her own time.

Leaving Nancy to her canary yellow paint, Liz strolled around the circle. Lance had cut the fruit into geometric shapes, which he was painting in garish colours. Polly, who had surprised Liz with her raw talent, had chosen to paint the fruit in different shades of purple. Sylvia was more used to making trinkets than painting, so she was copying Polly. Trevor had painted his canvas black and was building up the colour to create depth. Catherine was painting a literal fruit bowl in watercolours and had even added in her own tablecloth along with a kitchen backdrop. Debbie had taken a similar approach to Lance and was using curious colours. Her banana was blue, and her apple was pink. Her bangles rattled from her cumbersome strokes, which appeared clumsy and unrefined.

Liz returned to her stool and continued with her own work. She rarely second-guessed her art. She never cared if people understood, or even liked what she created. She enjoyed the process of painting. Before the police, Liz had studied fine art at university. She had switched paths when she realised her passion would not pay the bills. Now that she was a forty-two-year-old woman with her own shop, she did not have to worry about her art earning her money. Instead, it was a way to relax, and it was much cheaper than therapy.

The shop's artificial lighting replaced the sun

after it set. When Trevor left the shop to answer a call, Liz knew the group was coming to its natural end. She always set a starting time, but never a finishing one. Sometimes they painted for an hour on the coast, and sometimes they worked for three or more hours in the shop. On one occasion, they had painted until midnight, none of them having realised how the time had flown.

"A *blue* banana," Catherine said with one of her usual forced smiles, which never seemed to go above her nose. "How *unusual*, Debbie."

"An ode to Picasso's blue period," Debbie replied as she stifled a yawn. "Not that *you* would appreciate it. Another pretty watercolour, I see. You do know how to stay in your little box, Catherine."

Before Catherine retaliated, Trevor burst into the shop, his phone clasped to his chest. He looked as though he had received the worst news of his life, which caused Liz to rise from her stool. She stretched out, her brows tightening as Trevor staggered back to his spot.

"Will Katelyn still be in the gallery?" Trevor asked Catherine, who also worked at the gallery with Nancy. "I need to speak to her – *now*."

"She's in Australia," Catherine replied as she packed up her watercolours, which looked immaculate thanks to her soft style. "She's visiting her parents for the month. If you need to ask something about the gallery, she's left me in charge until she gets back."

"That *witch*!" cried Trevor before punching a hole through his painting. "I'm going to *kill* her when I get my hands on her!"

Lance, who had been the only one still painting by this point, looked up, blinking his way out of his art trance. Trevor stumbled away from his ruined piece, stopping when he fell into a display of knitting wool. Half a dozen bundles fell off the shelf, scattering at his feet. Nancy caught Liz's eye, one of her brows arched above her glasses.

"What's happened?" Debbie walked over to Trevor, her bangles clanging as she rested her hands on his shoulders. "*Breathe*, Trevor. Think about your blood pressure. You're going to have a heart attack if you keep this up. It's the biggest killer of men in their fifties."

The threat of a heart attack snapped Trevor out of whatever rage he had entered. He blinked around the group, remembering where he was and what he had done. He stared down at his ruined piece, and then down at the paint on his knuckles, regret in his gaze. He ran his hands over his bald scalp, his shirt pulling out of his waistband to reveal the bottom of his potbelly.

"Have you ever heard of Murphy Jones?" Trevor asked, looking at the group as he steadied his breathing. "The artist?"

"Murphy Jones?" Lance replied, his attention on Trevor. "Of course I've heard of Murphy Jones! One of the greatest landscape artists of the last century, if not of all of time. His work fetches millions at auction. It's so rare because he didn't paint in volume, but what he did paint was technical perfection."

"Jones?" Nancy echoed, looking at Liz. "Any relation, Liz?"

"Do I look like a woman drowning in millions?" Liz replied with an awkward laugh. "It's a common surname."

"Well, Murphy Jones was no common man," Catherine said, her tone different from the one she had spoken about Picasso with. "He was a *genius.*"

"And so is Katelyn," Trevor mumbled, his gaze

distant as he stared at the bowl of fruit in the middle of the room. "She's sold me a couple of fakes."

"*Fakes*?" Lance stood up, his hands disappearing up into his messy bun. "Oh, man! You're in trouble. How did she get her hands on those?"

"I don't know," Trevor whispered. "She came to me with them, and I thought they were stolen. She needed them off her hands, so she gave me a good deal."

"You bought *stolen* art?" Debbie cried, stepping back from Trevor as her ringed fingers drifted up to her mouth. "That's blasphemous, and not to mention highly illegal!"

"I'm a collector," Trevor snapped, regarding Debbie as though she had said something unusual. "How do you think valuable art moves around the world? It doesn't come up for sale like a pair of old shoes, Debbie. And as it turns out, I *haven't* bought any stolen art. I bought two exceptional fakes from a very skilled saleswoman."

"How do you know they're fake?" Catherine asked through pursed lips as she stared over her glasses at Trevor. "Katelyn isn't the nicest woman, but she's not a criminal."

"Isn't she?" Debbie scoffed. "I went to art college with her. She's a despicable creature!"

"There's a guest at the hotel claiming to be an antique expert," Trevor said as he gathered up his things. "I need to speak to him right now. What if he's wrong? He must be. *No one* can fake a Murphy Jones."

"How much did you pay for them?" Nancy asked as though she was getting the latest juicy gossip on something trivial.

"Half a million," Trevor said, his cheeks burning bright red. "*Each.*"

A gasp shuddered around the room, only broken up by Lance, who seemed to be finding the whole thing amusing. He shook his head as he chuckled to himself, his muscular arms tight around his chest.

Trevor ran to the door without saying goodbye. He jumped into his expensive sports car, its wheels skidding on the road before taking off.

"Any man that has a million to spend on fake paintings has *too* much money," Lance announced. "Capitalism is the root of all evil, and Katelyn Monroe is as evil as they come."

"*Evil?*" Catherine scoffed as she pulled her coat

on. "I'm sure it's a mix-up. She's an honest woman. I work with her every day."

"As do I," Nancy mumbled, her tone less favourable.

"She's a *snake*!" Debbie cried, her voice cracking at its height. "I wouldn't put *anything* past her!"

Liz kept her opinions on Katelyn Monroe to herself. When she had first moved to the town, Nancy had encouraged her to take her art to the gallery to have some of it displayed. Liz had not been very optimistic about her chances, and she had been right not to be. Katelyn had cut her down in seconds, making her feel like she should never dare pick up a paintbrush again. It had affected her for a single afternoon, but she was not going to let the opinions of an uptight manager get to her.

"Would this be a bad time to suggest we put on an exhibition of our group's work at the gallery while Katelyn is away?" Nancy suggested with a sheepish smile as she stared through the hole of Trevor's ruined work. "It would be fun."

"Sounds like the perfect protest to me," Lance agreed as he assessed his own work. "It might be our only chance to have anything displayed in that gallery.

Katelyn is a heartless dictator."

"I'll think about it," Catherine said in a firm tone that Liz knew meant '*it's a no, but I don't want to say no yet*'. "It doesn't *quite* work like that."

"Surely it's a simple case of taking some pictures off the walls to put some more up?" Debbie muttered with a roll of her eyes before staring up at the ceiling. "Can anyone smell smoke?"

"It's the burnt rubber from Trevor's tyres," Catherine said confidently. "He set off at some speed. Do you know if The Sea Platter is still open? I'm starving."

Liz looked at Nancy, who seemed to click onto what Liz was thinking. They shared a look of pure panic as their joint gaze flicked upwards, and then to the door. Setting off as fast as Trevor's car, Liz skidded into the street. Paddy followed, her sudden movement waking him from his nap behind the counter. She looked up at her flat window where small curls of dark smoke were forcing their way through the cracks.

"*The biscuits*!" Liz and Nancy cried at the same time.

Liz opened her front door, without stopping to

check if the handle was hot. She darted up the stairs, her breath leaving her body when she saw orange flames spitting out of the oven. They had engulfed the kitchen faster than seemed possible.

"What do we do?" Nancy cried, her sleeve covering her mouth. "*Oh, Liz*! Didn't you set a timer?"

Liz remembered the fire extinguisher behind the counter downstairs. She jumped down the entire staircase before bursting out into the street again. Debbie held Paddy back by his collar while Catherine rang for the fire service on her mobile phone. Liz snatched up the red extinguisher from behind the counter and sprinted back up the stairs. She pushed past Nancy, not thinking about her own safety as she ran towards the flaming oven.

Liz wrenched on the safety tag, pointed the hose at the blaze, and sent thick foam onto the flames. For a moment, it did not seem to do anything, so she moved closer, the temperature crackling against her face. It was only when the canister of foam had almost emptied that the blaze died down. Liz dropped the extinguisher to the floor as she cleared her lungs. The burnt husks of the cookies taunted her through the smashed window of the oven.

“I told you I can’t bake,” Liz said to Nancy with a sheepish smile.

Two

Hurrying down one of Scarlet Cove's winding backstreets, Liz sniffed at her coat's collar. It had a strong scent of smoke like everything else in her flat. She made a mental note to find out from Nancy if Scarlet Cove had a launderette tucked away somewhere. Despite having lived there for six months, the town kept revealing itself to her like a magic eye picture.

"Liz!" Nancy called, waving from the steps of the

gallery. "Excited about your debut?"

"I think so," Liz replied. "I'm quite nervous, to tell you the truth."

Liz could barely believe she was about to see one of her paintings on a gallery wall, and she was even more surprised that it was at Scarlet Cove's gallery. Nancy's suggestion to exhibit their groups' work had rapidly come to life, despite Catherine's protests that Katelyn would blow a fuse if she found out.

In the week since Liz's kitchen fire, Nancy had pulled the opening together at lightning speed. She had proven that she paid attention from behind her reception desk. Liz had offered to help to take her mind off the damage she had caused with her misjudged baking, but Nancy had everything under control. All Liz had had to do was select a piece for the exhibit, and turn up on time.

"Sorry I'm late," Liz apologised as she gave her sleeve a cautionary sniff. "I was trying to drown this coat in perfume."

"You smell like a barbequed gardenia," Nancy replied with a wriggle of her nose. "I quite like it."

"Well, that's something."

"I can't believe you're insisting on staying in that

flat," Nancy said as they headed for the gallery. "My sofa is comfortable and vacant."

"My bedroom is fine," Liz said. "It's just a little smoky."

Arm in arm, they walked into the gallery. There was an unusual buzz in the air as chatter and music drifted down from the main exhibition room. Liz avoided the gallery as often as possible, but she was sure the small group milling about in the reception area alone was the busiest she had seen it.

"You're never going to believe the turnout," Nancy whispered to Liz as she nodded to the door of the main gallery. "Everyone has turned up."

Liz gulped hard, the thought of her fellow townsfolk seeing her work a daunting prospect. She wondered if it was too late to pull her painting to replace it with something safer and less revealing.

"It's a bit of fun," Liz said with a self-assured smile, brushing her red curls away from her face. "It's not a real exhibit, is it? Not really. We didn't earn those spots on the wall. We're only doing it because Katelyn isn't here."

"Well, for not a '*real*' exhibit, it's the most attended since I've worked here," Nancy said with a shrug. "If I were in charge of this place, I'd put your piece on the wall in a heartbeat."

"You would?"

"You're a brilliant artist, Elizabeth Jones," Nancy said with a wink. "And I'm not saying that because you're my best friend. I've been telling Katelyn for years that she should include more local artists on the walls, but she doesn't listen. She's so stuck in her ways. She reminds me five times a week that she's the one with the fine art degree, and I'm the receptionist."

"You could rule the world," Liz said, knowing it was her time to be the reassuring friend. "If that gallery is as full as you say it is, it's only because you've worked your backside off organising this whole thing."

Nancy fiddled with her glasses, a proud smile on her face as her cheeks flushed bright pink. They set off down the corridor towards the gallery, the chatter growing louder with every step. When Nancy pulled open the door, Liz's heart skipped several beats. Nancy had not been exaggerating about the turnout.

It seemed the majority of Scarlet Cove had turned up to see the local art. It only occupied one of the long walls in the gallery but was the only one demanding any attention. Liz nervously scanned the faces, relieved when she spotted some of her art group in the middle of the room taking turns answering questions. Despite wanting to observe from the edges, Liz found herself walking over when Debbie beckoned her with a jangle of her bangles.

"Isn't this amazing?" Debbie squealed as she clasped her ringed fingers around Liz's arm. "I've waited for this moment my whole life."

"Enjoy your time in the sun," Catherine said with a strained smile as she peered over her glasses. "Katelyn will return and put things right."

"And until that horrid moment, I'm going to soak up every ounce of glory," Debbie said, her mood too high for Catherine's pessimism to bring it down. "People seem to be loving my piece."

Still clutching Liz's arm, Debbie nodded to her giant canvas, which was in the middle of the wall. She had chosen a psychedelic painting of a rose, which she had painted in textured acrylic. Liz spotted a couple of people tilting their heads at the painting before shaking them and walking off. She was glad when Debbie did not seem to notice, and if she did, she was not showing that she cared.

"I bet this is the first time this gallery has had any real art on the walls," Trevor scoffed after a deep glug of champagne. "I'd bet my fortune that the rest of those classics that Katelyn Monroe adores are fake too."

"No luck with the Murphy Jones pictures?" Lance asked, trying to hide his amused smile.

"*Fakes*!" Trevor exclaimed with a small burp from the bubbly. "Both of them are completely worthless! I couldn't sell them for scrap money, even though they're great fakes. The only chance I have is to dupe someone the way Katelyn duped me."

"You should destroy them," Debbie said with a heavy shake of her head. "The forger stole a talented man's ideas. You need to do the right thing."

"And what about my money?" Trevor cried, sloshing his champagne over Catherine's grey blazer, turning it dark charcoal. "I'm down a million. It will take me months to recover."

"*Months*?" Lance mocked. "You poor thing. Why don't we get a collection plate going 'round while everyone is here? I'm sure we could help you recoup your losses if you keep that pathetic look on your face."

Trevor did not take Lance's bait, instead choosing to follow a young woman holding a tray of appetisers. Chuckling to himself, Lance headed off in the opposite direction. Catherine also darted off when she noticed a boy reaching up to touch one of the classics on one of the other walls. Debbie joined another group of women when she heard them discussing her painting. Realising she had not even seen her own work on the wall yet, Liz pushed her way through the crowd with a polite smile, Nancy right behind her.

When they broke through, they joined a little old woman who was staring up at Liz's painting through thick glasses. She lifted a finger up and wagged it at the painting.

"This is my favourite," she exclaimed with confident certainty. "It would look lovely in my dining room. Are they for sale, Nancy?"

"Not this time, Doris," Nancy said with a badly concealed grin. "But I'm sure I can put you in touch with the artist. She'd love to paint a commission for you."

Doris said that she would like that very much before shuffling along to the next painting, which was Nancy's fruit bowl from the last group meeting. Doris shook her head before immediately moving on. Liz and Nancy stepped back and stared at Liz's painting in silence for a moment. Liz had painted it almost three years ago, and it was the piece she was most proud of, even if it did expose her soul.

"I didn't get it at first," Nancy said as she looked at the tag under the picture. "'*Lovers Lost*'. It's Lewis, isn't it?"

Liz nodded as she stared at the fragmented face of her late husband through layers of white fabric fluttering in a non-existent wind. She had painted the picture after waking up in the middle of the night after dreaming about him days after his funeral. The dream had been so vivid; the paintbrushes had done the work for her. In the dream, Lewis had been right in front of her, looking back with a smile, but she had not been able to wade her way through the fabric to get to him. When she had awoken in the morning, she had thought the painting had been part of her dream until she had seen it staring at her from the bottom of the bed. It made no logical sense, and yet it perfectly spoke for itself. Whatever her style was, this was not it, but it was the piece she cherished the most.

"It's beautiful," Nancy whispered as she wrapped her hand around Liz's. "It's my favourite too."

Liz squeezed back, suddenly feeling tears coming from deep within. She forced them down, not wanting to reveal even more of herself to the spectators.

"Cheese nibble?" a familiar and comforting voice breathed into her ear as a silver tray appeared in front of her. "I've been looking for you."

Liz spun around, never happier to see Simon's dimpled smile in front of her. He kissed her on the cheek, sending the tears back to where they had come from. In his white shirt and tie, and his apron wrapped around his waist, he looked as handsome as ever. Liz gladly tossed one of the nibbles into her mouth.

"You scrub up well for a farmer," Nancy said with a wink as she grabbed a nibble. "I should go and check that everything is ticking over."

Liz had got used to Nancy disappearing every time Liz and Simon were in the same room together. Almost-kisses and awkward conversations had tainted the first three months of their relationship. Yet, the past three months had been some of the happiest Liz had experienced, and that was because of Simon. She had moved to Scarlet Cove with the intention of leaving her pain behind in the city for the sake of having a future. Falling in love with a handsome thirty-four-year-old cheese farmer had not been in her plan.

"These are delicious," Liz said as she picked up another nibble, realising how hungry she was after skipping breakfast thanks to her useless kitchen. "You have a talent for cheese."

"Brie with cranberry sauce on a small rye cracker," Simon said with a pleased and proud smile. "I thought I'd go a little fancier with my cheese talent to compliment your amazing painting talent."

Simon looked at the painting, a squint in his eyes as he tried to figure it out. Liz blushed as she reached for another brie and cranberry rye cracker. Nancy had managed to extract Liz's past from her, but Simon did not know a thing. Despite him often asking about her pre-Scarlet Cove life, she avoided concrete answers. She hated the thought of Simon feeling second-best to a ghost. She still had love in her heart for Lewis, but it did not make her love for Simon any less real. Would he understand that after she had kept the secret for six solid months?

"Who's the dude?" Simon asked, nodding at the picture.

"A man I saw in a dream," she answered quickly. "I still haven't wrapped my head around this whole thing."

"I saw a woman taking a picture of it on her phone earlier saying it had inspired her to take up painting again," Simon said, his grin as proud as when Liz had complimented his cheese nibbles. "You really are phenomenal, Liz Jones. Is that a new perfume? You smell different."

"Eau De Smoke," Liz joked in a mock French accent. "I'm still living in the ashes of my cookie catastrophe."

"What?" Simon cried, his eyes bulging. "I thought you said Bob Slinger was fitting a new kitchen this week?"

The mention of her landlord sent the hairs sticking up on Liz's neck. Bob Slinger was a short man with a bulbous nose who reminded Liz of a beardless Santa Claus in looks and personality. When she had called to let him know what she had done, he had found the whole thing rather amusing and seemed to only care for her wellbeing. In his own words, 'kitchens are replaceable', not that he seemed to be in any rush to replace hers. Anyone else would grow tired of her daily calls, but Bob Slinger answered heartily with '*any day now*' when she asked for an update on the arrival of the new kitchen.

"I'm sure it'll be sorted soon," Liz said, giving her sleeve another sniff; the excessive perfume was wearing off, and she could definitely smell smoke. "I'll be fine."

"The offer still stands for you to stay at the farmhouse," Simon said. "In fact, my parents are insisting."

"I'm not a damsel in distress," Liz replied with a smile. "But I appreciate the offer."

"That's what I told them," Simon replied with a wink. "You're a tough cookie, Liz Jones, but there's no shame in accepting help. We have a spare bedroom made up for guests, and even if it's only for a couple of days, you'll be out of the way for when the new kitchen needs fitting."

Liz was about to decline the offer again when a woman walked past, her nostrils twitching in the direction of her smoky coat.

"Do you have a washing machine?" Liz asked, her cheeks blushing when the woman gave her a disapproving look before disappearing into the crowd.

"Of course," Simon whispered, planting his hand on Liz's shoulder. "And a tumble dryer. Just say yes, Liz."

"But I have Paddy."

"And I live on a farm," he replied with a laugh. "Ellie will love having him around. You know how my little sister loves that dog. It might even be fun to see each other every day. Just nod your head. Give in!"

Before Liz realised what she was doing, she nodded her head. She was not sure if it was the promise of clean clothes or the offer of spending more time with Simon that persuaded her, but she felt sudden and unexpected relief about not having to endure another night sleeping in what felt like a bonfire.

"That's sorted then," Simon said before giving her another peck on the cheek. "I'll call my mum now. She'll do a backflip. I think she loves you more than she loves me."

Liz scooped up another appetiser before Simon

weaved his way through the crowd with a spring in his step. Liz had spent a lot of time at the farmhouse over the last couple of months. She preferred being with Simon there rather than her small flat. She loved the wide-open spaces and beautiful views, which stretched all the way to the water's horizon. Simon's parents, Sandra and John, were the loveliest people Liz was sure she had ever met. They were traditional farmers down to the core. They had embraced and encouraged Liz and Simon's relationship from the start. Liz also enjoyed the company of Simon's seven-year-old sister, Ellie, with whom she had bonded. She was vivacious and funny, with unexpected emotional intelligence for someone so young. Liz chewed another nibble as she stared at Lewis' face.

"Who would have thought I would end up here, eh?" she whispered with a soft chuckle. "I hope you can see me wherever you are."

Leaving her painting behind, Liz turned and looked around the crowd for some of her art group. She spotted Poppy and Sylvia chatting animatedly in a corner, but the rest, including Nancy, had vanished. Popping the last nibble into her mouth, she turned to find her group again. She stopped and almost choked on the small piece of cheese when she spotted a tall, slender woman standing in the doorway, a black suitcase next to her. Liz forced the cheese out of her throat, her cough sending a shudder of silence across the gallery as everyone else noticed the arrival of the woman.

"It looks like I returned *just* at the right time," Katelyn Monroe shrieked, her crystal blue eyes bulging out from her tanned face. "What on *Earth* is going on in here?"

Three

The gallery manager took a step forward, leaving her suitcase in the doorway. Everyone stepped back as though a hungry lion had wandered into the gallery. Katelyn looked around the room, her icy gaze landing on the wall of local art. Her eyes popped even further out of her face, her lips disappearing into a tight line. Catherine hurried into the gallery behind her, almost tripping over the suitcase.

"*Katelyn*!" she cried, trying to inject lightness into her shaky voice. "You're back a week early. Aren't you a lovely colour? How was Australia? I hear it's lovely this time of –"

"*What* is going on?" Katelyn's refined voice repeated, her eyes homing in on Catherine. "What is that *ghastly* flower mess doing in the Turner spot?"

"*Ghastly*?" Debbie cried, dumping her champagne flute on a waiter's tray after emerging from the crowd. "How dare you, you little –"

"It's a *temporary* exhibit," Catherine said as she grovelled at Katelyn's side. "It was all Nancy's idea. *She* did this! It was going to be back to normal before you returned. I swear!"

"I left *you* in charge, Catherine!" Katelyn cried, her eyes widening as she took in the unusual paintings on the wall. "I cannot bring myself to look at them. They're *hideous*. You know how I feel about modern art."

"I know, Katelyn," Catherine said, almost begging for forgiveness by her boss's side. "I'm sorry. Let me fix this."

"Get them off the wall," Katelyn ordered, a hysterical shake in her low voice. "Right now!"

Nancy walked into the gallery room, followed by Lance. Nancy looked terrified when she spotted Katelyn in the middle of the silent gallery. Lance seemed amused by the manager's untimely arrival. Liz caught Nancy's gaze and mouthed '*sorry*', hoping it would ease the fear in her friend's eyes; it did not.

"I said *now*!" Katelyn shrieked.

Catherine scurried forward, cramming her glasses on the end of her nose. She pushed through the crowd as if it was not there, her only thought to fulfil Katelyn's demand.

Firstly, she took down her own watercolour painting of the harbour, then Trevor's gothic interpretation of Scarlet Cove Castle. It shocked Liz that Catherine had bent to Katelyn's will so easily, especially since she was so defiant and unapologetic when it came to her own opinions.

"People are enjoying the exhibit," Nancy mumbled as she fiddled with her glasses, her fear of Katelyn muffling her usually loud voice. "It's something different."

"I don't want *different*," Katelyn snapped, the suggestion turning her tanned cheeks red. "This is a *classic* art gallery. We display *real* art, not this nonsense."

"It's not all about you, Katelyn," Debbie cried, stepping forward so that they were face to face. The manager's slender frame made Debbie look like a stout hobbit. "You've *always* been the same way. You should *never* have got this job."

"And you should?" Katelyn snarled back with a smirk. "Get out of my sight, Debbie Downer. Go and throw some paint on a canvas and call it '*art*'."

Liz thought she might have to pull Debbie off Katelyn, but the insult seemed too much for her. She ran to the door, her excessive jewellery clattering in the awkward silence.

"Give it a rest, Katelyn," Lance said, his voice deepening as he rubbed the lines on his forehead. "Look around. People *were* enjoying themselves."

"This is a place to *respect* and *admire* art," Katelyn snapped, barely looking in Lance's direction. "If you all want a party, go to that gaudy cabaret bar and congratulate each other for picking up a paintbrush there."

Liz opened her mouth to defend what they were doing, but no words came out. She looked around the full gallery, and she noticed others doing the same.

Katelyn's presence was so strong, it filled every corner of the room, sucking out the oxygen in the process. Only a brave few seemed able to challenge her. Liz's blank mind and frozen tongue stopped her.

After struggling with Debbie's large piece, Catherine moved onto Liz's painting. She huffed and puffed as she tried to remove the artwork, but '*Lovers Lost*' did not budge. Liz wanted to call out to demand she be careful with the work, but the words would not come.

"It's stuck," Catherine said meekly when she noticed Katelyn staring at her. "It's jammed on something."

Katelyn pushed through the crowd, shouldering Liz in the chest as she passed. She shoved Catherine out of the way and stared at the painting with disdain before prying her fingers behind the frame. She wriggled it, the wood bending this way and that. When it finally came free, it did so with consequence. The splitting rip of canvas echoed around the room, followed by a shudder of gasps and mumbling. Katelyn tossed the ripped art onto the floor as though she was discarding a banana skin. She dusted off her hands, pleased with herself. She scanned the gallery as though daring anyone to challenge her. Her eyes landed on Liz for a moment, making her wonder if she knew it was her art.

"I'm going to my office to see what other messes you've caused," she said through gritted teeth to Catherine. "When I come out, I want everything back to how it was. Do you understand me?"

Catherine nodded like a naughty schoolchild, despite being twenty-years Katelyn's senior. Liz could feel Catherine's embarrassment as they watched the maniacal manager storm through the crowd. She grabbed her suitcase and vanished. Liz turned to Catherine, sure she was holding back tears behind her glasses. Seconds later, she scurried to a door on the far side of the gallery.

"Oh, Liz," Nancy whispered, gripping her hand as the crowd made their way towards the door. "I'm sorry."

Liz stepped towards the canvas on the floor, a jagged slash cutting down the middle of Lewis' face. She knew it would be irreparable. She looked up at the wall and spotted the culprit: a stray bent hook. Liz forced her breathing to slow down, pushing forward a strained smile after a heavy blink.

"It's only a painting," she said firmly, despite the ache in her chest. "I can paint another one."

Nancy squeezed hard, not knowing what to say. As the gallery emptied, Simon forced his way back through with a fresh tray of appetisers. He scanned the gallery with a confused look before catching Liz's eyes.

"What have I missed?" he asked, ditching the tray on one of the wooden benches in the middle of the room. "Why are all the paintings on the – Oh, Liz! What happened to it?"

"Katelyn happened," Nancy said tightly. "I need to go and make sure I've still got a job to come back to tomorrow."

Nancy plodded off, her head low. By the time she reached the door, Liz and Simon were alone in the gallery. Thanks to the now empty wall, the abandoned room seemed double the size. She looked at the paintings on the floor, dancing past her own; she could not bring herself to look at it again.

"Katelyn did that?" Simon asked, casting a finger to the painting. "Who does she think she is?"

"The manager," Liz said with a sarcastic laugh. "As first exhibits go, it was certainly eventful. I hope the local paper reviews it favourably."

Simon pulled her over to the bench where they sat on either side of the tray of cheese nibbles. Liz tossed one into her mouth as she looked around the empty gallery. One of her lifelong dreams had come true and had been shattered in front of her eyes within the same hour.

"How are you so relaxed right now?" Simon asked, his hand wrapping around Liz's. "I didn't even paint it, and I'm fuming."

"There's no point crying over a ripped painting," Liz said calmly. "That's how the saying goes, isn't it?"

"She *can't* get away with this!"

"She has."

"Report her," Simon said, suddenly sitting up straight. "Call the police and tell them she vandalised your property."

Liz considered the proposition for a moment. She still had enough contacts in the police to make Katelyn's life uncomfortable for a couple of weeks, even if she knew it would never lead anywhere. Even if they could bring about charges, which would never happen, it would not un-rip the painting. Despite telling Nancy she could paint another one, she knew she would never try.

"It's just a silly picture," Liz said firmly. "There are more important things in the world. How did your parents take the news?"

Simon pursed his lips, but he did not challenge Liz, something he had learned would not lead anywhere. Years of being a detective had given her a skill for avoiding questions when she wanted to. She had witnessed enough slimy criminals doing the same in interviews.

"They're more than happy to have you for as long as you need to stay," Simon said as he looked down at the plate of cheese. "I wonder if I'm still going to get paid for this."

"I wouldn't hold your breath," Liz said. "I'm guessing Nancy didn't make a contract?"

"Not quite," Simon said with a shrug. "I was giving her mate's rates anyway. I should clear up and get back up to the farmhouse to make sure Mum and Dad aren't putting up welcome banners. See you tonight?"

"You can count on it," Liz said, letting Simon kiss her on the cheek. "See you later."

Simon scooped up his tray and with a wave,

exited the gallery. Liz stared at the blank wall. She did not know how much time had passed before Catherine hurried in with a trolley holding the classic art that originally belonged on the wall. Catherine ignored Liz as she restored them to their proper homes, treating the artwork on the floor with more respect than her boss had. She carefully stacked them up and put them on the trolley, wheeling them into the room she had presumably been in since the exhibit's demise.

Liz stared at the dark paintings on the walls in their heavy gold frames. She appreciated most art, including the '*classics*', but Katelyn seemed to be obsessed by the dullest examples of bygone eras. Between the standard landscapes and un-smiling portraits, Liz could feel her passion for art draining by looking at them. Knowing it had been Katelyn who had chosen them, and that she had been the one to destroy Lewis' portrait, her delayed anger rose up.

"Who does she think she is?" Liz mumbled to herself, jumping up and immediately marching towards the door.

Liz turned left, remembering where Katelyn's office was from the day she had foolishly thought the manager might have displayed her work. That had been during Liz's first week in Scarlet Cove, but she was no longer naïve when it came to Katelyn Monroe. Her frozen tongue had finally melted, and she knew exactly which piece of her mind she was going to give her.

Liz marched right up to the door, pausing for a moment, her knuckles clenched over the mahogany wood. She looked at the brass plaque with Katelyn's name on it. Liz decided she was not going to give Katelyn the choice of ignoring her. Unclenching her fist, she reached out for the doorknob. She twisted and pushed forward.

"*Elizabeth*?" a familiar and refined voice called down the corridor. "What a lovely surprise!"

Liz pulled the door back into its place, turning to see Christopher Monroe, a local business tycoon and owner of Scarlet Cove's harbour. Unlike his sister, Katelyn, Liz liked Christopher, despite their early interactions revolving around his unrequited crush on her. She noticed the deepened tan on his face and the whiteness of his blond hair, and realised that she had not seen him about town for the last couple of weeks.

"Australia?" she asked, pushing her momentary

rage away. "You look well."

"As do you," he said as he gave her an awkward hug, his tailored suit pressing cumbersomely against her. "Thankfully, I was able to cut my trip short. The thought of spending another week with my parents was rather frightful."

From what Christopher had told her about his parents, she was not surprised. A team of nannies and cooks had raised him while his wealthy parents indulged in their fortune. They had lived in Australia for many years, and Christopher had not seen them since. They only communicated via phone calls to ask if their forty-something-year-old son had married yet.

"I hope you had a nice time," Liz said, glancing back at the office door, small talk the last thing on her mind. "Did you take any good –"

Before Liz could finish her sentence, a tall and beautiful woman walking through the reception area distracted her. She had the face of someone in their early thirties and the body of someone a decade younger. Slender and toned, yet still impossibly curvaceous. Her hair was golden blonde in tight ringlet curls, and her complexion buttery and bronzed. She reminded Liz of an early Kylie Minogue album cover. When the beauty spotted the back of Christopher's head, she revealed a full set of beautiful pearly teeth, like a shark after a trip to the dentist. To Liz's surprise, she slipped her arm around Christopher's, her eyes landing on Liz.

"Here you are," the model-like woman said, a definite Australian twang to her voice. "I've been looking everywhere."

"I wanted to check something with my sister," Christopher said, resting his hand on the strange woman's soft fingers as he stared awkwardly at Liz. "Elizabeth, this is – well, this is also, Elisabeth."

"With an '*s*'," the Australian beauty announced, extending a hand. "Elisabeth Wilson. Everyone calls me Lizzie. Nice to meet you, Elizabeth."

"Everyone calls *me* Liz," she mumbled, confusion clear in her voice. "It's very nice to meet you."

Liz accepted Lizzie's hand, noticing the giant rock on her left hand. Christopher noticed that she had noticed and smiled sheepishly, his cheeks turning a deep shade of red.

"This is my fiancée," he announced flatly. "I'm finally getting married!"

"Our parents know each other," Lizzie explained,

her grin widening as she looked up at Christopher. "We met at the beginning of his trip and fell madly in love, didn't we?"

"Yes," Christopher replied, as though someone had asked if he wanted a cup of tea. "Is my sister in her office?"

Liz stared down at the ring again, confused by what was standing in front of her. She remembered seeing Christopher in The Sea Platter less than a month ago, and he definitely had not been engaged then. She wondered if she had bumped her head during the exhibit, hoping the last eventful hour had been nothing more than a horrible concussion. When Lizzie locked her dazzling green eyes on Liz, she knew her feet and mind were planted firmly in reality.

"I think so," Liz said, hooking her thumb over her shoulder to Katelyn's office door. "I wanted to speak to her myself, actually."

Christopher let go of Lizzie's arm and walked around Liz to the door. He knocked, but no one answered. The two women stood next to each other, their smiles awkward and the air silent. Liz wondered if Christopher had told his new fiancée about his exhausting pursuit of Liz when she first moved to the town.

"Katelyn?" Christopher called through the wood. "It's me. Do you have my passport? I can't find it, and I don't want to accept that I've been silly enough to leave it in the taxi."

Christopher looked over his shoulder at the two women, smiling stiffly as he waited for a response. When he did not get one, he grabbed the door handle as Liz had, pushing open the door. He stepped inside, his footsteps clumsy and rigid. Liz stepped forward to follow him inside, but the Australian pushed past her, keen to stick to her new fiancé like Velcro.

There was a moment of uncomfortable silence before Lizzie let out a blood-curdling scream. It echoed down the empty corridor, piercing Liz's ears from every angle. Lizzie buried herself into Christopher's chest, her gigantic diamond glittering under the light. Liz stepped into the office, her breath escaping her when she saw what had made Lizzie scream.

Katelyn Monroe lay limply across her desk, her feet and hands hanging over the edges; she was obviously dead. A fabric curtain tie around her neck confirmed the cause of death, but that was not what had caught Liz's attention. Instead of seeing a pale face with bright blue lips and bulging eyes like every other strangulation victim, an explosion of colour greeted her. Vivid paint covered every inch of Katelyn's dead face as she lay on her desk, an unmoving and empty piece of art. Christopher stumbled backwards, the weight of his distraught fiancée pushing him into the wall. He reached out and grabbed Liz's arm, his crystal eyes wide, his lips parted but unable to speak.

"Christopher," Liz whispered, the words catching in her own throat as she scrambled for her phone to call the police. "I'm so sorry."

Four

"Is that all you're bringing?" Simon asked, cocking his head at the two carrier bags and backpack Liz had with her.

"I travel light," Liz said with a smile. "Come on, Paddy."

Simon took the bags and headed towards the farmhouse, Liz close on his heels. Before she followed him, she looked over Scarlet Cove as the setting sun stained the clear sky pink. The macabre thought that it looked like Katelyn's frozen face drifted through her mind. Before her mind's eye could focus on the gallery owner's body, her attention wandered to the harbour on the coast's edge. What was Christopher doing right now? She had wanted to talk to him, but after the police had interviewed them all separately, Lizzie had whisked him away.

"Penny for your thoughts?" Simon asked, his voice soft and soothing as he rested a hand on her shoulder.

"I'm thinking about how great it will be waking up to this beautiful view," Liz said, the lie obvious in her voice. "I don't think I could ever get used to it."

Simon kissed her on the top of her head before wrapping his arm around her. They stood and watched the sunset for a moment. Liz had never been more grateful to have her caring farmer boyfriend than in that moment. Years as a detective had never taken the edge off seeing a dead body, especially when it was someone she had known.

"Mum's made up the guest room for you," Simon said, his soft grin so infectious that Liz could not help but mirror it. "Are you ready for the welcome party?"

"Ready as I'll ever be."

Simon pushed open the door into a small stone vestibule. Paddy ran in as though he had lived there his whole life. Simon passed the bags to Liz as he kicked off his dirty wellingtons on the doorstep.

"I need to wash these off," he said, nodding for her to venture in alone. "They don't bite."

"I know," Liz said with a nervous smile as Simon walked around the farmhouse, leaving her alone.

Liz swallowed down the nerves as Paddy barked before spinning around in a circle. She told herself to stop acting like a teenager. She had walked into the farmhouse alone on many occasions over the last couple of months. A quick glance at the bags reminded her why she was nervous. She had lived alone for so long now, she was not sure how she would react to having a full house around her.

"Come on, boy," she said as she reached out for the handle. "I'm being silly, aren't I?"

Liz stepped over the threshold, the heat from the rustic kitchen warming her in seconds, banishing the chilly February air. Her cheeks flushed, forcing her to unravel her yellow knitted scarf. Paddy darted forward, his nose taking him straight under the giant table in the middle of the room, his nails scratching against the red tiles.

No matter how many times Liz visited, she could not help but look around the vast kitchen in amazement. Every appliance was a different colour from a different era. They clashed with the plates, plaques, and horseshoes cluttering the exposed dark stone walls. Pots and pans hung from the low-beamed ceiling over the square table in the middle of the room, its wooden surface looking as old and used as the farmhouse itself. The chairs around the table were different shapes and sizes, but it added to the character in a way that would only work in a farmhouse. Unlike her own shell of a kitchen, it was homey and lived-in. She could almost smell the years of casseroles that the stove had cooked.

The sound of Liz closing the door behind her brought Simon's parents, John and Sandra, bustling into the room. She did not doubt they had been waiting in the other room anticipating her arrival.

"We heard you found *another* body." Sandra cried before pulling her into a tight hug. "You poor thing."

"Give the girl some breathing room, Sandra," John said in his deep, booming voice, his grey moustache dancing on his top lip. "Let her get her coat off at least."

Sandra was wearing her usual floral apron, which she had fastened over a fleece. Tight-fitting brown jodhpurs tucked into riding boots completed the look, making her look like she was ready to jump on the back of a horse at any moment. John was wearing a black Barbour jacket over a checked shirt, which was tucked into faded jeans. A flat cap balanced on top of his thinning hair. Liz was sure if she looked up '*typical British farming couple*', a smiling picture of Sandra and John Greene would be proudly displayed.

Sandra let go when Liz returned the hug. After months of living in Scarlet Cove, hugs from locals had become part of common practice when it came to greetings. She was slowly growing to like them.

"I know we mustn't speak ill of the dead, but Katelyn Monroe wasn't a nice lady," John announced as he pulled off his flat cap. "I hope she rests in peace though. We all deserve a chance to try on old age."

"Is it true what they're saying about her painted face?" Sandra asked, the gossip channels in Scarlet Cove connected all the way up to the farm on the hill. "How bizarre."

"Unfortunately, yes," Liz confirmed in a formal procedural voice she had not heard leave her lips in a long time. "Although it was less children's party, and more a statement."

"Who do you suppose killed her?" John asked, his finger tapping on his chin. "Odd way to go."

"I don't know," Liz lied, not wanting to admit she already had her suspects lined up in her mind and they all belonged to her club. "Thank you for letting me stay here. I do appreciate it."

"We'll hear none of that," John said with a hearty chuckle. "It's our pleasure! Ellie has been so excited since she heard you'd be here."

"Besides, you're practically family!" Sandra announced as she ushered Liz over to the kitchen table to sit down. "The minute I clapped eyes on you, I said to my John that you and our Simon would end up together. Didn't I say that, John?"

"Let the woman settle in, Sandra."

"But I *did* say that," Sandra whispered to Liz before shuffling over to the metal kettle on the stove. "I'll make us all a nice cup of tea, and we can have a nice chat. I can't tell you how much this place needs another woman." Sandra filled up the kettle before igniting the gas hob with a match. "With all this work at the farm, I don't get to town much. I need to catch up on the gossip."

John gave his wife a stern look, but it softened in a second, and a look of realisation struck Sandra's face.

"What a *terrible* thing to say!" Sandra scolded herself, placing her hand on her chest. "Considering what has happened, gossip is the last thing this town needs. When will I learn to think before I speak?"

"Don't be silly, my dear," John said, giving her such an endearing look that Liz could not help but smile. "You're perfect to me."

In all her years of living with her parents as a child, Liz could not remember them ever sharing a tender moment. Both being lawyers, their conversations revolved around work, their language formal and coded. Sandra and John seemed so in love, even after so many years together. Liz knew that she would be a lucky woman if she were as happy as they were when she reached their age, which she was realising was not as far off as it seemed.

"While you're here, this is your house too," Sandra said as she scooped loose tea into a china teapot before pouring in the boiled water. "We want you to feel right at home, don't we, John?"

"What's ours is yours," John said, spreading his hands out like a circus ringleader as he bowed to Liz. "Don't be afraid to ask. We're more than happy to accommodate your needs."

"I've always said you were a hotel owner in a previous life," Sandra said as she hurried over with the teapot. "John loves nothing more than a house full of people."

Before Liz had time to say a word, Ellie ran into the room, her blonde pigtails fluttering behind her. She jumped onto Liz's lap, hugging and winding her in the same moment.

"*Liz*!" she cried breathlessly, her little hands wrapped around Liz's neck. "Come and see my room first! You *have* to see all my teddies. I even called one Liz."

"Tea first!" Sandra cried as she poured Liz a cup. "Sugar and milk?"

"No, thank you," Liz said as she returned Ellie's tight embrace.

"This woman is made of strong stuff," John said with a friendly slap on Liz's shoulder. "I like her more and more every day."

Ellie slid off Liz's lap, her attention immediately turning to Paddy. She zoomed towards him, her arms outstretched. Paddy noticed just in time to escape, running out of the kitchen. After a few moments, Liz heard Paddy's fast footsteps echo down the hallway followed by Ellie's. Simon slipped inside, shoeless with his clean boots in his hand. He dropped them onto an already full shoe rack next to the door before flashing Liz a grin.

"How are they treating you?" Simon asked with a wink. "Hope they're going easy on you."

"Of course we are!" Sandra exclaimed as she sat across from Liz, a cup of tea in her own hands. "You know we love her, Simon. Maybe even more than you do."

"Not possible," Simon said before kissing Liz on the top of her head and sliding into the seat next to her. "What a day. I've put the horses to bed, and the chickens are all fed. Cows need sorting out, but I needed a sit down after today."

"You put your feet up," John said as he slapped his flat cap back on his head. "I've got it."

John slipped out of the kitchen, leaving Sandra to

grab another cup for Simon. They sipped their tea and chatted about what had been happening in town, the conversation strangely staying away from the gallery murder. Liz was sure the only thing worse than having to talk about it was not talking about it at all. When Ellie zoomed back into the room, Liz was almost glad of the distraction. Her cheeks were flushed and stray strands of hair had fallen over her face.

"Come see my room," Ellie demanded, tugging on Liz's sleeve. "*Please*!"

"I hope you have the energy to keep up with her," Sandra said with a soft chuckle. "She's a little ball of lightning. She runs circles around us."

"*Please*!" Ellie begged, tugging even harder. "Please, Liz!"

"Let me show Liz her room, and then I'm sure she'd be happy to," Simon said after draining the last of his tea. "Wouldn't you, Liz?"

"I'd love to," Liz said as she ruffled Ellie's hair. "I hope it's nice and tidy."

With Simon's help, Liz pulled off her coat and hung it on a hat stand next to the overflowing shoe rack. Simon picked up the plastic bags and Liz picked up the backpack. They looped their free hands together before he led her out of the kitchen and into a narrow hallway.

"Sorry about them," Simon whispered, his grip tightening around her hand. "They get over excited."

"They're sweet," she said as they walked down the hallway lined with family pictures leading back to before Simon was born. She paused at a picture of Sandra and John on their wedding day standing outside St. Andrew's Church. They looked as happy today as they did then. "I would have killed for parents like yours when I was Ellie's age. They disliked me the second I expressed any interest in art."

"How could anyone dislike you?"

"Ask my parents," Liz replied with a forced laugh. "It's a wonder I turned out this normal."

"Well, I wouldn't go *that* far," he joked. "But I'd love to meet them one day."

"One day."

The rest of the farmhouse was as lived in and homey as the kitchen. She had visited quite a few times since her and Simon's first kiss but rarely ventured past the kitchen. They usually spent their time in Simon's separate cottage, which was on the farmland but removed enough to feel like its own home.

They stopped when they came to a small, oak door at the end of the hallway. Paddy scampered past them, his tongue lolling in excitement as Ellie pursued him, almost knocking them both off their feet.

"It's a bit small," he explained almost apologetically as he opened the door. "But I think it'll be comfortable enough for you."

Liz looked at what would be her new home for the next week or so and instantly loved it. The curtains and the fresh bedding were both white with powder blue detail. The light oak furniture added to the lightness of the space. It reminded her of a bed and breakfast, and was exactly how she had imagined her own room would look before moving to Scarlet Cove.

"It's perfect," Liz said, stepping in and dropping her bag on the bed. "I love it."

Simon walked over and placed the carriers next to Liz's backpack. He tweaked at the curtains, his cottage coming into view in the distance. The suggestion to stay there together had not come up. Liz wondered if it was because Sandra and John had traditional views or because Simon was respectful. Either way, she liked that they had allowed her to have her own space for the duration of her stay.

"If you need help, you can send me a Morse code signal," Simon laughed as he let the curtain drop into place. His eyes darted down to a sketchpad that had fallen out of the plastic bag and onto the bed. "Working on anything good?"

Simon flicked through a handful of sketches before landing on the page Liz hoped he would skip past. He turned it the right way up, homing in on Katelyn's name in the middle, with the names of her art club leading from it.

"I know what you're thinking," she said, her tone defensive. "But I *know* it's someone from the club, I just don't know who."

"You've put Nancy's name here," he said, his brows furrowing together. "She's not a murderer. How can you be so sure it was someone from your group?"

"I have a feeling."

"Oh, Liz," Simon said with a frown. "Maybe you should leave it to the police this time? I know you're more than capable of figuring it out, but after what happened at Halloween, I couldn't bear anything happening to you."

"Nothing will happen to me," she said as she took the sketchpad from Simon before snapping it shut. "It's only notes. My mind was working overtime while I was packing so I scribbled them down to get it out. I'm not going to do anything with it, but it doesn't take away from the fact someone *did* kill Katelyn at the opening of an exhibit featuring *my* club's art. Who else would even have a motive?"

"She wasn't popular, was she?" Simon replied. "Anyone could have done it."

"And the paint?" Liz tossed the sketchpad onto the bed and crossed her arms. "It's a statement, most likely revenge for something, and the art group isn't exactly lacking motives after she ruined our opening."

Simon sighed heavily, and for a moment, Liz thought he was going to walk out of the room, leaving her alone with her notes. Instead, he wrapped his arms around her waist and pulled her in. He stared deeply into her pale eyes, his gaze softening.

"You really care about this stuff, don't you?" he whispered.

"Old habits die hard."

Simon leaned in and kissed her on the lips, and for that brief moment, the murder melted away. Ellie appeared in the doorway, bursting the blissful bubble.

"*Ew!*" the little girl exclaimed with a screwed-up face. "That's gross!"

Simon gave her a stern look, causing her to giggle and dart off again, Paddy trailing behind. A rapturous chorus of '*Liz and Simon sitting in a tree*' echoed down the narrow corridor.

"Well, at least one good thing has come from this," Simon said as they both sat on the edge of the bed.

"What do you mean?"

"Nancy will be keeping her job after all," Simon replied. "She was distraught when Katelyn fired her."

"Fired?"

"Didn't she tell you?"

"I haven't seen her since the gallery."

"Oh," Simon said, his cheeks blushing as though he had said something he should not have. "It's not my news to tell you, but after I'd finished talking on the phone with my parents, I went to fill up my cheese tray. On my way back, I saw everyone leaving the gallery. I bumped into Nancy. She was sobbing. She said Katelyn had fired her for being the one behind the exhibit. I'm sure she was going to tell you, not that it matters now. She might keep her job after all."

Liz did not like the uneasy thoughts that were flooding her mind, but she tried to subdue her suspicions. Even though she had written Nancy's name as a suspect, it had been a technicality because she was part of the group.

"Don't," Simon said. "Just don't."

"Don't what?"

"Think Nancy killed her!" Simon cried, suddenly standing up. "I've known her my whole life. *You* know her, Liz. She's not capable of something so horrific, and don't think for a second that she is."

"I know," Liz said, her tone unsure. "It's a process of elimination."

"A process that belongs to the police," he reminded her. "And last time I checked, you like reminding people of your *retired* status."

Before they could talk about it any further, Ellie and Paddy returned to whisk Liz away so she could finally meet her teddy bear counterpart. After a pretend tea party in the little girl's bedroom, Sandra came in to put Ellie to bed, much to her disappointment. Liz's assurance that they would continue the tea party tomorrow seemed to settle her, leaving Liz to return to her bedroom alone after turning down Sandra's invitation to join them in the sitting room by the fire for a game of gin rummy.

When she was alone in bed, she turned to the suspects list with a freshly sharpened pencil grasped in her hand. Using the soft glow of the bedroom lamp as her guide, she thought back to what Simon had revealed to her and wrote it down word for word.

"Oh, Nancy," she whispered to herself, her writing taunting her. "I hope I'm wrong about this."

Five

A couple of days after moving into the farmhouse, Liz was surprised when her art group turned up for their regular meeting at her shop. She was less surprised when Catherine and Nancy were the only two not to show their faces. Liz had not seen either since Katelyn's death and was beginning to think they were purposefully lying low.

Liz had not prepared anything, so they trotted down to the coast to paint the last of the evening sun before it faded. Liz set them up next to the harbour in hopes of seeing Christopher, but his office was locked up. A sign in the window announced, '*CLOSED DUE TO FAMILY BEREAVEMENT*', in stark black ink that left Liz feeling a little cold.

Sandwiched between Debbie and Lance, Liz tried her best to slip into her special place; it did not happen. She had settled on an uninspired composition, her colour choices were obvious, and her strokes were clunky. More than once, she caught herself staring at Christopher's office. When Debbie announced that she was cold and wanted to go home, Liz was more than happy to cut the group short.

When Debbie and Lance wandered off in one direction, and Polly and Sylvia in another, Liz realised she had missed her chance to interview her suspects covertly. She wondered if the police had questioned any of them yet, or if they had not made the connection as quickly as she had. The group had been surprisingly quiet, and none of them had mentioned the ruined exhibit or the murder, which was suspicious in itself. With only Trevor, the owner of the Scarlet Cove Manor Hotel, not in a hurry to leave, the fake paintings sprung to Liz's mind.

"Do you still have those paintings?" Liz asked, forcing her tone to stay casual. "I was wondering if I could have a look at them? I've never seen a real Murphy Jones before. I suppose this is as close as I'm going to get to one."

To her surprise, Trevor did not deny her request to see the fakes. They loaded their equipment and unfinished paintings into the back of his car before driving up to the hotel.

Like Simon's farm and Scarlet Cove Castle, the manor hotel sat atop the hill looking down over the sloped coastal town. Liz had never visited, but she had passed it on many occasions during her evening strolls with Paddy. By the time they pulled up in front of the hotel, the sun had completely set, but the dusk did not take away from its beauty. It was perfectly symmetrical with a long balcony inserted in the middle. In the dark, it was beautifully lit, bringing out the moss and ivy that grew neatly on the walls. The large stone building was the perfect holiday spot for those with a little more money to spend.

"My great-great-grandfather built it in 1853 as a holiday home for the family," Trevor explained as he jumped out of his car, which he had parked next to a bright pink Range Rover. "It's been passed down from generation to generation. It was my father who turned it into a hotel."

"It has the wow factor," Liz said as she climbed out to join Trevor in looking up at the building. "I bet this would be fun to paint."

"You're more than welcome to come up and give it a go," Trevor said with a polite smile. "I've tried, but I never quite capture the scale of the place. It looks even more beautiful in the summer."

Liz followed Trevor through the grand entrance and into the reception area. An ornate sweeping mahogany staircase commanded attention in the centre of the space. It took Liz's breath away, but Trevor wandered into the room as though he was walking around an empty space. He had no doubt seen the beautiful view every day since he was a little boy.

"I still have them displayed in the sitting room," Trevor said as Liz followed. "I may as well try and get my money's worth out of them."

The sitting room was a majestic room with windows on three of the four walls looking out over the beautiful grounds. A fire roared in the grate of a giant fireplace, the armchairs and sofas angled in its direction. Two elderly women were enjoying tea by the flickering flames, both looking at the new arrivals before returning to their conversation.

"I still can't get over the shock of finding out they were fake," Trevor said as he stared at the two giant landscapes. "They look so real."

Liz stepped back and looked at the paintings. They were so clear and photorealistic it took her a moment to recognise that they were even paintings. One depicted a forest, but the composition focussed the attention on the setting sun above the treetops. The other was a shot of the countryside, captured in winter with grey and blue tones. Both were so different, and yet their technical perfection was breathtaking. Liz had studied Murphy Jones' work at university, but she had never come across either piece before.

"They're stunning," Liz whispered, stepping closer to the paintings, which were so large, they swallowed up most of the wall. "*How* can these be fakes? The detail is extraordinary."

"It's easy to spot if you know how," announced an unfamiliar male voice from behind them. "Even if they are perfect examples of excellent forgeries."

Liz turned to see a tall, handsome man in his mid-sixties staring at the paintings. Like Trevor, he had his shirt open at the collar, but unlike Trevor, his body was rather trim, and he had a full head of thick greying hair. From the clothes he was wearing, Liz could tell the man was wealthy. He flashed her a toothy, charming smile, which she could not help but return. The stranger had an instant likeability and warmth to him that few people had.

"This is Brian South," Trevor said, motioning to the tall man. "He's the expert who spotted that they're fakes."

"I'm no expert," Brian said. "I'm merely a simple antique dealer enjoying a holiday by the coast. It's lovely to meet you –"

"Liz Jones," she said as she shook the man's hand. "It's nice to meet you."

"Jones?" Brian said, arching a thick brow with a smirk. "No relation to the famous Murphy, are you?"

"Not that I know of," Liz answered as she turned back to the paintings. "You said it was easy to spot fakes if you know how?"

"It's all in the dates," Brian said, stepping back as

he hooked his thumbs into his jeans pockets. "Murphy Jones lived an extraordinary life. He was born in 1884 to David and Jacqueline Jones, but they both died in a factory fire not long after, leaving him an orphan. He was raised in an old Victorian workhouse before they were outlawed. When he was eighteen, he moved to the Cotswold village of Peridale, which is where I was born and raised, although our paths never crossed. I may be old, but I'm not *that* old. He became an apprentice of the famed Peridale painter, Donald Clapton, who like Murphy, was a brilliant landscape artist. I think even Donald would have agreed that his apprentice outgrew his talents.

"When a lot of people think of Murphy Jones, they think of his Yorkshire landscape paintings from his later years. He didn't achieve fame for his work until the 1940s, and he was about my age by then. Few know that he lived in Peridale between the ages of eighteen and thirty-two. He had a natural talent from the start, and he painted a lot during his time in Peridale, that was, until he was enlisted in the army to fight in the First World War. Unlike his paintings, he survived the war. Nobody knows what happened to his work from those years. He painted infrequently during his famed period, but when I was a child, there were enough people around who remembered Murphy Jones. They say he was seen constantly painting, and he was amazing at it. He'd sell them to locals, but like anything without any perceived value, things go missing and get destroyed. That's why when one of his pre-war paintings does show up, they sell for a lot. I've known one to sell for over a million pounds at auction."

"I should have known it was too good to be true," Trevor said with a roll of his eyes.

"You're not the first to be duped by a fake Murphy Jones," Brian said, patting Trevor on the shoulder. "In fact, you're not the first to be duped by *that* specific forgery." He pointed at the wintry countryside painting. "I saw *that* myself this past July. Caused quite a lot of trouble back in Peridale. The best man at both of my weddings, Anthony Kennedy, stole that painting from his lover thinking it was a real Murphy Jones. He hid it in plain sight, knowing all about the one that sold at auction for over a million. He made the mistake of telling his mother about it, not thinking she would know the significance. She was old enough that her timeline had crossed with Murphy Jones'. Their relationship wasn't good enough for her to spare his life."

"His mother murdered him for a painting?" Liz asked, her detective senses pushing forward. "I read about that in the paper."

"It made the national news," Brian said with a roll of his eyes. "She poisoned him with arsenic, hoping she could steal the painting for herself to keep her cosy in her retirement, not that she could find the thing. He owned a coffee shop in the village and hung it on the wall, knowing most had forgotten all about Murphy Jones. It's funny what the promise of money can do to people. People have killed for that painting, and it's not even real. I have no idea how it ended up down here."

"You still haven't explained how you know they're fake," Liz said, feeling uneasy in the presence of the wintry countryside. "If they're so rare and valuable, how can anyone tell?"

"Because that was painted in the 1930s, not before the First World War," Brian said confidently. "It's all in the colours. They're not contemporary to the period they're claiming to come from. These were painted by another famous man from Peridale, an art forger named Martin Edwards. I've seen his handiwork more than once. These pictures have no real-life counterparts that have been discovered. Martin was also an incredibly skilled artist himself, but he was a chameleon. He could copy people's styles as though he had their hands. He painted a batch of Murphy Jones paintings in Peridale in the 1930s. I've looked at photographs of the landscapes and the trees from that period, and they match up with what he recreated in Murphy's style. If they had been real Murphy Jones', the landscape would have looked subtly different. A lot can change in twenty years.

"Martin's little enterprise made him a rich man before he was caught and imprisoned. His grandson was Anthony's lover, and he'd kept hold of the fake. He never knew the truth of his grandfather's forgery past, and it cost him his life. Anthony's mother also poisoned him with arsenic when she realised he might work out the true value of the painting to try and steal it back. Aside from Anthony, he was the only person who knew what the painting looked like until I noticed it on the coffee shop wall. Of course, it was all too late by then, and the coffee shop closed immediately after. I went back to give the painting to the authorities, but it had vanished."

"Sounds like you live in an eventful village," Trevor exclaimed. "I'm glad Scarlet Cove is quiet."

"Peridale has its moments," Brian said with a dark chuckle. "Although I overheard someone talking about a beheading here at Halloween? My daughter is quite the amateur detective. I'm sure she would have figured that out in a matter of days."

"It *was* figured out," Liz said almost defensively, not mentioning that it was her who had put the pieces together. "Do you have any idea how Katelyn Monroe could have got hold of these paintings to sell?"

"It's not difficult," Brian said with a subtle shrug, his eyes trailing to the window. "Art, especially stolen art, moves quickly and smoothly through underground channels. There's usually a chain of people involved with putting people in contact with buyers. You might have handed over a million pounds for the pair, but I doubt she kept even half of that. She would have taken a finder's fee, but that's likely all." He waved to the window, his attention suddenly divided. "Listen, I need to go. We're going to dinner with some friends, and we're checking out first thing in the morning. I wanted to thank you for a great stay and to apologise that you've been the one to end up with these paintings. If you want my advice, keep them and don't let them pass around anymore. There's too much blood on these paintings already."

Brian shook their hands before heading for the door. Liz looked out of the window at a platinum blonde woman who was wearing a very revealing outfit. She held a baby in her arms who could not have been more than a couple of months old. At first, Liz thought the young blonde must be the antique dealer's daughter until he kissed her on the lips before they both climbed into the bright pink Range Rover.

"Lucky fella," Trevor said with a sigh. "Married a girl twenty years younger than him. We should all be so lucky, right?"

Liz smiled uncomfortably, her age-gap with Simon suddenly shrinking into insignificance. She stared up at the wintry painting again, remembering Brian's comment about there being blood on the painting. She looked back at Trevor and wondered if his need to get his own back on Katelyn could have resulted in her death. Aside from his outburst at the art club the night of Liz's kitchen fire, he was usually mild-mannered, if not a little pompous and arrogant at times. Was he capable of murder?

"I should get going," Liz said as she checked her watch. "I promised Simon I'd be back in time for dinner. Thanks for letting me look at them. I know you've lost a lot of money, but they *are* wonderfully painted. Perhaps in another lifetime Martin Edwards was the famous painter, and Murphy Jones was the imitator?"

"That's a lovely thought, but I can't make any money from that, can I?" Trevor said, a hint of the anger she had seen from him before pushing through his deep voice. "I'm an art collector. I was going to hold onto them for a couple of years, and then sell them. They're worthless pieces of junk otherwise."

With that, Trevor stormed off, leaving Liz alone in the sitting room with the two elderly women. She smiled over at them, and they smiled back, no doubt having eavesdropped on their entire conversation. Leaving them to gossip about the scandals they had overheard, Liz headed for the door. She decided she would walk across the top road to the farm and enjoy the cool evening air. On her way to the exit, she spotted Christopher and Elisabeth being shown around the grand reception area by a staff member. They were arm-in-arm and taking in the details, relaxed smiles on their faces. Liz hung back for a moment, wondering if she could walk out before they saw her. When Christopher caught her gaze, he smiled and diverted their tour towards her.

"What a pleasant surprise, Elizabeth!" Christopher exclaimed in his usual posh voice, no trace of sadness at the recent death of his sister. "Are you taking a break from the town?"

"It's a flying visit," she explained, smiling awkwardly at Lizzie, who was even more intimidatingly beautiful than Liz remembered. "How are you?"

"Fine," Christopher replied, his lips smiling rigidly, but his pale blue eyes empty. "Absolutely fine. We're here looking at using this as a potential wedding venue."

"Wedding?" Liz asked, the words catching in her throat. "Isn't that a little soon?"

"We're in love," Lizzie said in a matter-of-fact voice. "There's no better time."

"I meant because of what happened to Katelyn,"

Liz said, her eyes imploring Christopher to drop the pretence. "It's only been a matter of days."

His eyelids fluttered for a moment, but his veneer did not shift. Lizzie pulled him in tighter, as though trying to remind him of something they had previously discussed. Liz wondered if she had been the topic of that discussion, or if she was reading too much into the look in Lizzie's eyes.

"We've set a date," Christopher said flatly. "We'll be married before the end of the month."

Liz almost protested. She wanted to see a flicker of grief from the man she knew was sweet and caring under the stiff-upper-lip attitude. Deciding it was a lost cause as long as he had Lizzie glued to his side, she gave up, making a mental note to catch him alone.

"I'm happy for you both," Liz said with a forced smile. "This is a great building, so you've picked well."

"I don't like it," Lizzie announced, her Australian accent sticking out like a sore thumb in the sea of British voices. "It's tacky. Don't you think so, Christopher?"

"Very tacky," he echoed. "I'll see you around, Elizabeth."

Christopher and Lizzie walked back to their guide, leaving Liz lingering by the desk. A young woman came over and asked how she could help, causing Liz to scurry for the front door. As she walked home in the dark, she could not shake one single thought from her mind. She did not trust Lizzie one little bit.

Six

Liz made her way from the farm to the gallery, bundled in her winter coat that now smelt of floral washing powder rather than smoke.

Her visit to the Manor hotel the previous day had revealed a lot about the history of the paintings. An evening of research had confirmed Brian's story, but she was not sure where it fit into the broader picture, if at all. It put Trevor in the frame and confirmed that Katelyn was as dishonest as Liz had always suspected.

Despite his temper, Trevor did not strike Liz as the type of man who would be capable of strangling a woman to death.

As she walked through the small town, she picked up on an uncomfortable silence. It was something she had experienced twice since moving there, both after unexplained murders. She pulled her scarf tighter around her neck as she weaved down a winding street, eager to force out the chill. Little rain droplets pattered from the sky, so she was glad when the gallery came into sight.

She walked into the foyer and the heat inside replaced the nippy weather, but the relief did not last long. Her heart sank to the pit of her stomach when she saw that Nancy was not in her usual spot behind the desk.

"Good afternoon, Liz," Catherine called from the corridor leading to the main gallery and Katelyn's office. "How can I help you?"

Catherine tottered towards her, peering over the top of her glasses. Liz picked up on an imploring look in the woman's eyes that she suspected was a covert request not to bring up the murder. Deciding she would play along, Liz pushed forward her brightest smile.

"How are things?"

"Oh, you know," Catherine said with a wave of her hand. "What can I help you with?"

The repeated question let Liz know Catherine would rather she was not in the gallery. Remembering she had information to find out, Liz bit her tongue.

"Is Nancy here?" she asked, hoping to see her friend emerge at any moment. "I haven't seen her in a while."

"I'm afraid not," Catherine replied vacantly. "I heard she had come down with that nasty bug that's going around. I hope she gets better soon, but I can't have her in here infecting everyone. Not that we've been particularly busy since – well, you know. Anyway, it's probably for the best that we're quiet for a while. It's not easy being the receptionist *and* manager on my own."

Catherine gave Liz her signature unsettling smile that never quite reached her eyes. It reminded Liz of a wax figurine in a museum, and they had always scared her as a child.

"So, you're running this place on your own?"

"Is there anything else that you needed?" she

replied, ignoring the question, her fake smile not faltering for a second. "We are rather busy."

"But you said –"

Before Catherine could think up a response, a jingling headed their way. Catherine looked over Liz's shoulder and puffed out a breath through flared nostrils. Liz turned to see Debbie hurrying towards them, an excited smile on her face. She was bundled up in what looked like at least four different patterned scarves, with a woolly hat on her head. She had a stack of canvasses stuffed under her arm.

"Liz!" Debbie said as she attempted to flatten down her wild hair sticking out of her hat with her free hand. "What a nice surprise to see you here."

Liz smiled back, her eyes fixed on the canvasses under her arm. Liz wanted to warn Debbie that now was not the right time to approach Catherine. Before she could speak, Debbie flounced past, her scarves and skirt billowing behind.

"Catherine," Debbie called as the new manager set off back down the corridor, her tiny heels clicking on the polished tiled floor. "I need to talk to you about my artwork. It will only take a minute."

"Can't you see that I'm busy?" she cried, waving

her hands over her head. "I don't know how Katelyn put up with this."

Undeterred by Catherine's cutting tone, Debbie followed her all the way to the main gallery. Liz followed with a groan, knowing how fireworks could fly when the women did not see eye to eye. Considering Catherine's current mood, Debbie would be the one walking away burned.

"If you could look at them," she said, hopefully holding the paintings out. "I think you'll be surprised. I've been trying a different style, and I think they'd work."

Catherine's face contorted into something halfway between a smirk and a look of disgust as she glanced at the art.

"It's not what we're looking for," she replied. "It's *never* going to be what we're looking for."

"But I thought –"

"You thought what?" Catherine cried, her eyes bulging over her glasses like an angered owl. "You thought that because Katelyn was dead that I would take down a classic piece to put up your efforts. You seem to forget that I've been sitting next to you at Liz's art club for weeks. I know what you're capable of, Debbie. *I'm* in charge now, so there's no point beating around the bush. I'm sticking to Katelyn's *modus operandi* whether you like it or not."

Debbie's jaw flapped for a moment, tears collecting along her lash line. Liz wanted to reach out and pull the woman into a hug, something she rarely felt the desire to do. Debbie looked like she needed it. The only thing that stopped her was Debbie offering the paintings one more time.

"I thought you'd be different," Debbie said, her voice low and desperate. "I thought you'd be *fairer.*"

"Why?" Catherine snapped, her voice echoing around the empty gallery. "*Hmm*? *Fair* isn't giving everyone a shot. *Fair* is letting average artists know when they're not good enough to be displayed in a prestigious gallery. You shoot a horse when it's lame, you don't let it wander around on a broken leg. You had your *brief* moment of glory, if only for an hour. Go home, Debbie, and don't bring your work here again."

Liz stepped forward, ready to give Catherine a piece of her mind, but she shot her such a stern look that it transported Liz back to being in trouble in the headmistress' office.

"You're *just* like her," Debbie whispered, her tone darker than Liz had ever heard it. "You don't deserve this job. You got it by default. Playing it safe isn't art, Catherine. I hope you go to sleep at night knowing your '*art*' is as mundane as it comes."

Catherine's head recoiled into her neck, making her sharp features look even more bird-like. Liz prepared her ears for another barrage of insults, but Catherine marched through the both of them towards the office. Katelyn's nameplate had already been replaced with Catherine's.

"I thought it would be different," Debbie mumbled as she looked down at her work. "I thought it would change things."

Debbie hurried out of the gallery, her footsteps quickening the closer she got to the front door. Liz sighed and looked around the gallery, a small canvas painted in a familiar style catching her eye. She only had to squint to see that it was one of Catherine's delicate watercolours tucked away in the corner of the gallery. It was there, but not commanding any attention. Liz was sure it had not been there on the day of the exhibit.

Deciding nothing more could be gained from

hanging around, Liz headed for the front door. Her heart sank when she saw Debbie sitting on the steps and sobbing into her ringed fingers. Her canvasses were at her feet, discarded in a puddle as the light rain continued to fall.

Liz hurried down the steps and scooped up the canvasses, not wanting to see any work destroyed in such a way. She placed them at Debbie's feet before sitting next to her.

"I wouldn't bother," Debbie sniffled through her tears. "It's rubbish. You heard her."

Liz picked one of the smaller canvasses up and held it at arm's length, tilting her head. She was not sure what she was looking at apart from an explosion of coloured acrylics.

"I like it," Liz reassured her. "It's stylistic."

"That's a nice way to say it's crap," Debbie scoffed. "Good, but never quite good enough."

"No," Liz said, wrapping her arm around Debbie's shoulders. "It's *unique* to you. That's what's so brilliant about art. It would be boring if all art looked the same."

"She's a perfect clone of Katelyn," Debbie stated as she started to sniffle again. "Just as cold and mean.

She should change her name."

There was nothing Liz could say because she did not disagree. She had not even disagreed when Debbie had called Catherine's art mundane. Liz wondered if the power had gone to Catherine's head that quickly, or if she was as cold and icy as she had always come across. Liz had expected her to open up over the course of their art meetings, but she had yet to see any warmth behind the trouser suits.

"You can't let it discourage you," Liz said. "Galleries aren't important. Aside from our vanity exhibition, I've never been in a gallery either. Katelyn rejected me too, and Catherine would do the same in a heartbeat. People told me all my life that I couldn't make a career out of art, and you know what, they were right, but it never stopped me. Paint because you enjoy it, not because you want to get validation from it."

"I only want it to be appreciated," Debbie said, shaking her head, before covering her face with her hands. "I'm the *worst* at the art club. I'll never be as good as Lance, or you. Even Trevor is better than me, and Polly! Oh, Polly! The hairdresser who has never painted can paint better than me. You all make it look so easy."

"That's not true," Liz said with a wink. "There's always Nancy."

Debbie met Liz's eyes, and they shared a laugh for a moment, the tears vanishing in an instant. Liz gave her shoulder a reassuring rub, knowing it would take more than supportive words and a cuddle to change her mindset. Liz had been there too in her younger years. Debbie was a similar age, but she could not imagine what it would feel like to have so much self-doubt in her forties. The police force had ironed that out of her. When it came to hard facts and evidence, there was no room for self-doubt.

"Did you know Katelyn wouldn't even put Lance's work in the gallery?" Debbie said as she wiped the tears away. "And they used to be an item. I never stood a chance. Lance is good enough to go pro, not that he cares about money."

"Katelyn and Lance were an item?" Liz asked, her curiosity piqued. "When?"

"Oh, yes," Debbie responded, stifling her sniffles. "It was quite the grand love affair. It was a while ago now, but if you've lived around here long enough, you never really forget anything. It's ancient history by now. I can't quite remember when they split up, but I know it was messy."

"They're an odd match."

"Not when you know the full story," Debbie started, her voice lowering as she prepared to share the gossip. "Lance stood to inherit a large family fortune. We're talking *millions.* More than her own family is worth. His parents got rich selling fur coats before attitudes changed for the better. They made some bad investments around the same time, and they threw good money after bad. Lance never cared. He's been vegan for as long as I can remember, so he was probably over the moon when the business went bust. Katelyn, on the other hand, wasn't. She ended things soon after the well ran dry."

"How long after?" Liz probed.

"A matter of days," Debbie whispered after a dramatic pause. "He was *heartbroken.* I think he still is, but he hides it well. He's travelled so much to get over her, or at least to get away from her. He hated her guts, but he loved her more. I saw him yesterday in the Fish and Anchor. He was worse for wear. He's never been much of a drinker that I know of, but he was ordering triple vodkas. Shirley had to get some of the lads to take him home because he couldn't walk."

"Poor Lance."

Debbie nodded in agreement as she wiped away the last of her tears. Liz looked up at the bruised sky as the dark clouds stained the afternoon. She was unable to imagine Lance, who seemed such a free spirit, with a woman as unbending and dull as Katelyn Monroe.

"I should thank you," Debbie said after a moment of silence, a meek smile breaking through her sadness. "I can't remember the last time anyone listened to me. You're a good friend."

"Anytime," Liz said, giving her one last squeeze. "I mean that. You know where my shop is."

Debbie nodded her understanding as she stood up. She brushed down her maxi skirt, her bangles clattering in their usual way.

"Don't forget your work," Liz said, standing up and passing them back to Debbie. "Put them on *your* walls and forget this place even exists."

Debbie accepted her art before heading down the street, leaving Liz to digest what she had heard. She tried to think about how Lance had spoken of Katelyn, but it had never been favourable. She thought about what Debbie had said about him hating her, but loving her more. Had his hate taken over long enough for him to kill her?

After making a note on her phone to look into the relationship more, she walked across the town in the drizzle. By the time she reached the colourful row of Victorian terraced houses, the rain had soaked Liz's hair to the scalp. She could hardly wait for the ball of frizz it was going to turn into when it dried. After brushing it out of her face, she knocked on the bright orange door. It was not long before she heard shuffling from the other side.

"Oh," Nancy sniffed, her nose bright red and her voice faint in her clogged-up throat. "Hi, Liz. What are you doing here?"

Liz felt guilty for even doubting Nancy's illness. Her eyes were red and puffy, and her nostrils looked like she had done nothing but wipe them with tissues all week. Her skin lacked its usual peachiness, and her voluminous hair was limp and lifeless. Even though she had a blanket wrapped over thick pyjamas, she was shivering.

"Do you want to come in?" Nancy asked before running her sleeve along her nose. "I don't want to infect you."

"I've always had a strong immune system," Liz said, stepping inside before Nancy could change her mind. "It'll take more than a cold to knock me down."

"Believe it or not, I'm actually over the worst of it," Nancy said as she shuffled down the hallway in her fluffy slippers. "The vomiting has stopped at least, but I still can't taste a thing."

Nancy lumbered into the front room, making walking look difficult. She plopped herself onto her sofa where Liz could tell she had been sleeping. She flopped into the corner, half-lying, half-sitting.

Aside from the scattered tissues on the floor, her house was still impeccably clean. Like on Liz's previous visits to her friend's house, not one thing was out of place. She might have had scatter-brained, but she was particular about her retro-style house. Every room looked like it had been ripped out of a furniture catalogue from the Swinging Sixties. A re-run of an old soap was playing on the television, and it took their attention for a few moments.

Liz squirmed in her seat, unsure of how to approach Nancy's dismissal. She was not officially investigating, even if information did keep falling into her lap. If she were investigating, she knew honesty was the best tactic.

"Simon told me about Katelyn firing you," Liz said, making sure to assess her friend's reaction.

Nancy's eyes darted from Liz to the box of tissues on the table. She plucked out a fresh one before loudly blowing her nose.

"Why didn't you tell me?" Liz asked when Nancy did not say a word. "That's the sort of thing you tell your best friend."

"I've been ill," Nancy replied with a stuffy and exhausted laugh. "And besides, Catherine doesn't know. I called in sick when the gallery reopened. She didn't say anything other than '*come back when you're feeling better*'. It's not a big deal."

"A woman died."

"A *devil* woman," Nancy said after blowing her nose again. "I can't say I've shed a tear for her. Her final act on this planet was to fire me for daring to put on an exhibit for my friends. If she had stayed in Australia until she said she would, none of this would have happened."

"You mean she wouldn't have died?"

"Well, probably not."

Liz wondered if Nancy could hear herself speak. She was trying to edge her into showing her innocence, but everything she said pushed her closer to guilt. Liz tried to imagine Nancy pulling a curtain tie around Katelyn's neck. To her surprise, it was not so difficult to conjure up.

"Did you see anything the day of the exhibit?" Liz asked, deciding to keep trying. "Anything weird?"

"Is this what you came here for?" Nancy asked, narrowing her eyes. "You're supposed to bring grapes and flowers to sick people, not a police interrogation."

"I wanted to check up on you," Liz said. "I thought you were avoiding me."

"What if I was?" Nancy replied with a snap to her voice that Liz had never heard before. "I haven't left the house. My Jack is on holiday with his dad in The Lakes, and now my best friend thinks I *killed* a woman for firing me."

"Nancy, I –"

"I wasn't the only person there that day," Nancy said, rubbing her nose hard. "The whole town was there."

"So, you didn't see anything suspicious?"

"Talk to Lance," Nancy said bluntly. "He ran past me covered in paint about ten minutes before I heard that Australian woman screaming."

Liz nodded that she would speak to Lance, even though she wanted to keep talking to Nancy. She wanted to mend the rift between them, but she had a habit of digging deeper holes when she had suspicions. Nancy had been the second person, after her landlord, that Liz had met when she had arrived in Scarlet Cove. Since then, they had been firm friends. Their relationship had been fun, but there was now something sour between them; Liz did not like it.

"You should go," Nancy said, her eyes on the television as one of the soap characters slapped another. "I need a nap. I'm exhausted."

Without even waiting for Liz to get off the couch, Nancy dragged the blanket from under her and pulled it up to her neck. Liz stood up, not wanting to leave, but also not wanting to make things more awkward.

"I didn't mean to upset you," Liz said as she headed for the door. "Get well soon."

Liz waited by the door for a reply, but she got the cranking up of the television's volume instead.

Liz set off across town, her feet taking her to the front door of her flat. When she had the key in the lock, she remembered she was staying at the farmhouse. Wanting nothing more than to crawl into bed without any questions, she almost headed up to the flat anyway. She stopped herself. She would leave stinking of smoke, which would cause questions when she did decide to return to the farm.

On her way back to the farm, she saw Christopher and Lizzie on a bench under the shelter of a chestnut tree. Neither was paying attention to the other. Christopher was checking his watch while Lizzie examined her manicured nails. They did not look like the loved-up couple they appeared to be whenever Liz was around.

"What are you doing, Christopher?" Liz whispered to herself as she set off up the winding lane to the farm. "I hope you're not trying to prove a point."

Seven

"That's perfect," Liz said, smiling from behind the easel she had set up in the middle of the farmhouse sitting room. "Try to stay as still as you can."

Ellie giggled as she continued to fidget on the chair Liz had put her in. Liz sketched out the shape of her, but getting a little girl to sit still for long enough was a more difficult task than she had bargained for.

Once Liz was happy with the outline, she started

to mix the colours for Ellie's pale skin tone. She periodically glanced back at Ellie to make sure she was getting the proportions correct, but as usual, she slipped into her world.

"I need to pee," Ellie announced, pushing her legs together. "Really bad."

Liz glanced at the clock, and then back at the painting. To her surprise, almost two hours had passed, and in that time, Ellie had sat somewhat still enough for Liz to capture her. Her excitement at being painted by Liz stopped her running off to play with Paddy.

"Let's take a break," Liz said, rubbing her hand as she felt a cramp creeping up. "You've done a great job so far."

Ellie jumped down from the stool before skipping off to the bathroom. Liz took her moment alone to assess the painting, which was coming together quicker than she had expected. Tilting her head, she was proud of the likeness she had managed to achieve from such a squirmy subject.

"That looks great," Simon said, emerging out of nowhere. "You're good at this. Coffee?"

Without waiting for a reply, Simon handed Liz a

steaming cup. As though her body appreciated the timing of the caffeine, she let out an all-consuming yawn.

"Exactly what the painter ordered," she said before sipping the hot drink. "How's the calving coming along?"

"Betsy gave birth about fifteen minutes ago," Simon said after checking his watch. "He's a healthy sixty-two pound calf. The vet is checking him over now, but it all went according to plan. We need a name for him."

"How about Java?" Liz suggested as she stared down into the blackness. "Or Caffeine? This is good coffee."

"I bought it especially for you. I didn't go for the cheap stuff either. Top shelf only."

Liz chuckled as Ellie strolled back into the front room, pulling Sandra with her to look at the picture. Sandra, who had spent all morning on the farm with Betsy, was wrapped up in a thick scarf, hat, and gloves. Ellie climbed back onto the chair and resumed the exact position Liz had put her in.

"Well, would you look at that?" Sandra beamed as she planted her hands on her hips. "J*ohn*! Come and look at this."

John walked in from the kitchen in similar attire to his wife. He pulled off his gloves before sliding one of his arms around his wife's waist.

"You've got some serious talent, kiddo," John announced, smacking Liz heartily on the back. "Have you ever thought about selling these things? You could make a fortune."

"It's just for fun," Liz said, looking at the paintbrush but not wanting to resume with an audience. "But thank you."

"Let's leave the woman to finish," Sandra said, shooing John over to the couch. "I want it done so I can hang it up right away. Maybe you could do a family one next?"

"She's not a printer, Mum," Simon said as he sat next to his parents on the couch behind Ellie on the stool. "Let her finish this one first."

"I'm only *saying*!" Sandra said. "It would be nice to have one of all of us, that's all."

"Pretend we aren't here," John added.

Liz took one more sip of the coffee before placing it on the side table next to her. She did not mind them watching her from afar, but the thought of someone watching every brush stroke sucked out the fun. After dipping her brush into some white paint, she assured Ellie they would be done soon, not that she seemed to mind posing.

"Thank you for offering to babysit in a few days," Sandra said after almost half an hour of silence. "We haven't had a chance to go out for a while, and it's big winnings at bingo."

"It's not a problem," Liz said as she tried to mix the perfect colour for the natural highlights in Ellie's fair hair. "We had planned to have a night in anyway."

"You'll be a good girl, won't you?" Sandra moved her attention to Ellie who was sitting beautifully. "Of course you will be. You always are."

Ellie simply nodded, taking her position as a model very seriously. Liz painted for another half an hour or so as Simon's parents chatted idly in the background. The second she slipped back into her world, it was easy to tune them out and continue with her art.

"I think it's done," Liz announced as she dropped the paintbrush into the muddied water for the final time. "Want to see, Ellie?"

Ellie jumped down, pushing forward her widest grin. She ran to Liz's side, almost knocking over the easel. Simon wandered over and joined them in staring at the finished piece.

"It looks *just* like me," Ellie squealed in delight, as she excitedly clapped her hands together. "Mummy, Daddy! Come and look!"

Ellie jumped up on Liz's lap and threw her arms around her neck, her lack of front teeth showing as she smiled.

"Can I keep it?"

"I painted it *for* you."

"Wow, kiddo," John said as he looked at the finished piece. "Looks exactly like a photograph."

"Are you sure you don't want any money for it?" Sandra asked placing her hand on her chest. "It's *very* good."

"I'm sure," Liz said. "You've been more than kind enough to let me stay here."

"And we've told you, that's *our* pleasure," Sandra said as she stared at the painting even closer. "The detail is astounding. I don't know how you do it! I can barely draw a stickman."

"Where should we hang it, sweetheart?" John

said, lifting Ellie from Liz's lap. "How about outside your bedroom, so everyone knows where you live?"

Ellie and John walked out of the room hand in hand with the painting. The way Ellie looked up at her father filled Liz with so much warmth.

"She's such a sweet girl," Liz said, reaching out for the coffee and almost picking up the muddy paint water in the process. "You two show you can be parents at any age. It's not often you hear about people having babies in their – what must you have been? Your late fifties?"

Sandra and Simon looked at each other before turning to Liz with identical smiles.

"I didn't give birth to Ellie, dear," Sandra said with a chuckle. "It would have been a genetic miracle if I had. I started going through the change when I was forty-seven, and it lasted a whole ten years. You've got all that to come yourself, but it's not too late for you to – y'know – have babies if you wanted to."

Liz and Simon both blushed, both of them picking up on what she was hinting at. It was a conversation they had yet to have.

"What my mother is *trying* to say is that Ellie was adopted," Simon said, his cheeks burning even darker as he looked at Liz. "We've had her since she was a baby."

Sandra teetered to a bookshelf and picked out a huge bursting photo album. She sat on the sofa and patted the seat next to her. Liz sat down, but Simon perched on the chair arm.

"We've fostered over forty children," Sandra said as she flicked through the pages of smiling children. "After Simon was born, we knew we had a great love for children, so we decided we were going to put this farm to good use. A lot of the time, we were a halfway stop for children before they found permanent homes. We took in babies and teenagers, some for weeks, some for months, and some for years."

"The house was always full growing up," Simon said fondly. "I wouldn't have had it any other way."

"We still get Christmas cards and the odd visit from some of them," Sandra said before turning to the last picture. "Ah, here she is." Sandra pointed at a picture of a younger-looking Simon holding a blonde baby girl in his arms. "Naturally, we got old, against our will. We couldn't keep up with the conveyer belt of the system anymore, so when we took Ellie in, we knew she would be the last one. We fell in love with her, and we realised we couldn't part with her, so we adopted her. She felt like ours the second we held her." Sandra stroked the picture, her eyes crinkling as she smiled dreamily down at the photograph. "She knows where she came from, not that it matters. I've loved every child that has come through here like they were my own."

"You're a good woman," Liz said looking directly at Sandra. "You really are."

Sandra beamed at Liz, and for a moment, she looked as though she was about to cry. She looked down at her watch before snapping the album shut.

"Would you look at the time," she said, closing the book and placing it back on the bookshelf. "It's almost Ellie's bedtime."

Sandra left them alone in the sitting room, but they did not stay seated. Simon jumped up and held out his hand, a playful glint in his eyes.

"I have a surprise for you," he said. "Follow me."

He led her outside and to his cottage. When they arrived at the darkened cottage, Simon unlocked the door, but he turned back to Liz, his teeth biting his bottom lip.

"Close your eyes," he requested. "Just for a

minute."

Liz pouted before doing as she was told. Simon grabbed Liz's hand and led her over the threshold into his cottage. She was tempted to open her eyes, but she kept them closed.

"Can you see anything?"

"Not a thing."

Simon let go of her hand, leaving her by the door. She heard him running around the cottage, the sound of a lighter flint flicking half a dozen times.

"Surprise!"

She fluttered her eyes and looked around the small cottage, which was washed in the glow of soft candles. It was tidier than she had ever seen it, and there was a bottle of wine and two glasses waiting for them on the kitchen table.

"I thought I'd do something special for us," Simon said, his voice barely above a whisper. "I thought I'd see you more since you moved in, but you always seem so busy. I thought this would be a nice way for some quality time. And, it is Valentine's Day."

"It is?" Liz exclaimed, spotting the card and flowers on the kitchen counter. "I forgot! Oh, Simon.

I'm sorry."

"Don't worry," Simon said with a wink. "I forgot too. You can thank my mum for a last-minute reminder. It's been a while since I've had to think about it."

"It's beautiful," Liz said, touched by the effort Simon had gone to. "Thank you."

"There's a lasagne waiting in the oven," Simon said as he led her into the tiny kitchen at the back of the cottage. "Mum made it for us. I only have to warm it up."

While the lasagne heated up in the oven, they sat at the kitchen table with their glasses of wine. It felt like such a normal activity, and yet it was one Liz suddenly realised they had not done in a while. She appreciated Simon going to the effort to give them some romantic alone time.

They chatted idly about the farm, and Simon's cheese and ice cream company before the conversation inevitably turned to Katelyn Monroe.

"Found anything yet?" he asked after sipping his wine. "I suppose you're all over the case."

"I don't know what you mean."

"Come on, Liz," Simon said, raising his eyebrows.

"I know you."

Liz sipped her wine, wondering if it was worth trying to convince Simon otherwise. She had not exactly been looking into things, but she had learned more than a couple of things that had piqued her interest.

"I've been keeping my ear to the ground," she said before taking a huge gulp of wine. "I haven't found out much."

"What *have* you found out?"

Liz shrugged before sifting through her head trying to organise all her information.

"Trevor is furious about Katelyn selling him the fake paintings," she stated, tracing the rim of the wine glass. "I visited his hotel, and I spoke to the man who identified them. He seems wealthy enough, but it must sting to be a collector and be duped like that."

"There's Catherine too," Simon said as he peered through the oven door to check on the lasagne. "She jumped into Katelyn's shoes pretty quickly."

"So, I've not been the only one thinking about it," Liz said as she concealed a smile. "She's on my list. She's certainly continuing Katelyn's dictatorship of the gallery. Katelyn embarrassed her in front of the whole town, so there's a motive. There's Debbie too."

"Is she the bangle lady?"

"That's her," Liz said with a chuckle. "She has history with Katelyn. I know they went to college together, but I haven't dug any deeper yet."

"Do you still suspect Nancy?" Simon asked, his eyes locking on her seriously. "I called her this morning. She told me about your visit."

Liz took another big gulp of wine. She wished she could say either way, but she still did not know what to believe. Nancy was her best friend, but when it came to the facts, she knew she could not be emotional.

"She has the motive," Liz stated. "And she had the means and the chance."

"But it's *Nancy*," Simon said. "Nancy Turtle. She doesn't even kill spiders in the bath. She catches them and sets them free."

Liz knew that Nancy was a good person, but she had met a lot of good people over the years who had snapped and done something bad. It could take a split-second decision to change someone's entire moral code.

"There's Lance too," Liz continued, deciding to

divert the conversation away from Nancy. "I heard about his relationship with Katelyn. It wouldn't make too much sense for him to wait for so long, but there could be something more."

"It wasn't any old relationship," Simon said, his brows furrowing. "It was so long ago, but I've known him since we were kids. They were about two weeks away from their wedding."

"Really?"

"He adored her," Simon stated. "She was different back then, but it was all an act. I suppose you heard about how it all ended?"

"Debbie told me she left him when the money went up in smoke."

"There's more." Simon's eyes widened. "She finished things at his birthday party. They had a big bash at the manor hotel. Every single person in Scarlet Cove was there. Katelyn got drunk and got up on the stage with a microphone and called off the wedding."

"Wow."

"It tore the poor guy up," Simon continued. "She didn't just rip his heart out, she tore it in half in front of every person he knew. That's when he started travelling. I don't think he could face it all, so he didn't. When he came back, he was different. He made a little money from selling his art while he was away, so he rented the cottage down the lane."

Liz thought about the cottage. She had passed it many times when walking Paddy, but she had had no idea that was where Lance lived.

The topic of conversation drifted away from Katelyn when Simon served up the lasagne. After cleaning their plates, they cuddled up on Simon's couch with their wine. When he turned the television on, *Titanic* was playing on one of the channels, so they let it play.

When the iceberg stuck the ship, she heard soft snoring coming from Simon. She peeled herself from under him and placed a blanket over him.

"Sweet dreams," she whispered after kissing him on the forehead.

Spirits high from the romantic evening, she headed back to the farmhouse. Like her son, Sandra was also asleep with *Titanic* playing quietly on the television. Liz thought about going to bed to continue making notes about the case, but she was wide awake.

"Let's go for a walk," she whispered to Paddy as she clipped a lead onto his collar. "I fancy some fresh air."

She pulled on her coat and set off to the edge of the farm. After unlatching the gate, she squinted into the distance, the lights from Lance's cottage shining in the pitch black.

"We shouldn't," she said as Paddy looked up at her with his glossy eyes. "Should we?"

Paddy tilted his head, his floppy ears hanging from his head. Her curiosity getting the better of her, Liz set off in the direction of the lights. She knew it was late, but she could not help herself.

She reached Lance's cottage a couple of minutes later. It was like Simon's in that it was small and modest, but it seemed to predate any of the other buildings in Scarlet Cove. When she heard Lance's voice coming from inside, she knocked on the door. The curtains twitched immediately. Seconds later Lance opened the door. He was wearing a pair of paint-covered white linen trousers, but the paint did not stop there. He was naked from the waist up, his chiselled, tanned torso on display and also covered in paint. From the way he clung to the doorframe, Liz could tell that he had been drinking.

"Yes?" he slurred, his eyes struggling to focus on

Liz. "What do you want?"

"Hi, Lance," she said, already regretting her decision. "I was walking Paddy, and I saw your lights on, so I thought I'd see how you were."

Lance sloppily raised an eyebrow as he tucked his messy hair behind his ears. He staggered back and walked into the cottage, leaving the front door wide open; Liz took it as an invitation.

Photos and memorabilia from different countries lined his walls and surfaces, giving the coastal cottage an unusual feel that Liz quite liked.

"I hope I'm not interrupting anything," Liz said as she followed him into the small sitting room.

"I'm painting," he said bluntly.

Lance walked over to his easel, which he had set up in the middle of the room. Liz looked around him to see what he was working on, speechless when she saw Katelyn Monroe staring back at her. She was much younger than the woman Liz had known, and she was much more beautiful than Liz remembered. The most striking thing about the portrait was the carefree smile on her lips. Liz was sure she had never seen Katelyn smile.

But the painting chilled Liz to the bone. The

portrait was beautifully painted, but Lance had defiled it by adding garish red horns, along with blackening out her eyes.

"My best work yet!" he exclaimed before grabbing a bottle of what Liz recognised as gin. He swallowed the alcohol without wincing before slumping down on his clothes-cluttered couch.

"Well, take a seat then," he cried, pointing at a similarly clothes-covered armchair. "You've probably come to question me, haven't you?"

Lance swigged another mouthful of gin before hiccupping. He turned to the painting and let out a deep and sinister chuckle. Liz perched on the edge of the armchair, her hand wrapped tightly around Paddy's lead. He looked up at her as though to say, '*what are we doing here?*'; she had no response.

"I know about your relationship with Katelyn," Liz began. "I can't imagine what you're going through right now."

"You're right," he said taking another long swig. "You can't. Everyone really does know everyone else's business around here. Makes me wonder why I even came back."

Liz thought back to the man she had met during

her first art club meeting. Lance had been sweet and funny. Nothing had hinted at the inner turmoil he must have been feeling. She imagined it must have been easier to bury when the person he had been so desperately in love with had still been alive.

"I heard about the way she treated you," Liz said, trying to gauge his reaction. "That must have been difficult to live through."

"Not that it's any of your business," he said. "But yes, it was. I had my old friend gin back then, and I have it again now."

Lance laughed coldly as he looked at the picture again. For a moment, a gut-wrenching look replaced the coldness. He swallowed it down with more gin. Was he drinking to cope with the pain, or to forget about wrapping a curtain tie around Katelyn's neck?

"I'm pathetic," he mumbled as he slumped into the corner, the almost empty gin bottle following him to the floor. "It was always her. I could never get over her, no matter how many beautiful women I had in my bed. Katelyn had a different side to her that no one knew. She could be sweet." Lance's bottom lip wobbled for a minute, but the tears did not come. "She had these three little Pomeranians. Fluffy, Bear, and Cuddles. She treated them like her babies."

Liz tried to imagine Katelyn with three fluffy dogs, but the image would not appear. She wondered if the gin had begun to affect his memory, or if it were possible for Katelyn to have had a side only Lance had seen.

"I waited all this time," he said, his red-raw eyes looking deep into Liz's. "And for what? She's gone. I always thought we'd end up back together. It was *meant* to be."

Liz knew crimes of passion were common when it came to murders, and when it came to Katelyn, he was passionate. From the feverish brushstrokes of the horns and the blacked-out eyes, Liz could feel his deep-rooted confliction. Was that conflict enough to lead a man to murder the woman he loved because he knew she would never love him back?

Lance sprang up suddenly, making Liz jump. She pulled Paddy closer to her as Lance's shirtless torso filled the room, his messy hair casting his eye sockets in dark shadows.

"Time's up," Lance said before scooping up the gin bottle to finish the last mouthful. "I would like to grieve alone."

Liz did not hesitate. With Paddy by her feet, she hurried to the door, closing it tightly behind her. The glass bottle shattered against the wood seconds later, making her speed down the short garden path. She looked back at the cottage one last time before setting off back to the farmhouse.

Liz had always liked Lance, but she had seen a side of him that had scared her. It was not so much his actions because he was not the first drunk she had met, but rather his sudden change in personality. The way a person could switch from Jekyll to Hyde had always fascinated her, but in the case of Lance, it scared her. She would never have thought the handsome, talented artist could get blind drunk and smash a bottle against a door. It only made her think seriously about what else he could be capable of.

Was Lance so in love with Katelyn that it drove him to kill her? The thought sent a shiver down her spine, adding another burst of speed to her steps.

"That wasn't a good idea, was it, boy?" she whispered to Paddy when she was finally unhooking the farm gate again. "Why didn't you stop me?"

Eight

"*Two weeks*?" Liz cried as she stood outside her shop the next morning. "You said the new kitchen would be fitted by the end of *last* week!"

"At least," Bob Slinger said with a whistle as he rocked back and forth on his heels. "You know what it's like."

"Why is it taking so long?"

"Ordered it from China, you see."

"China?" Liz remarked.

"Yup," Bob said nonchalantly, pleased with himself. "I got a great deal! My eyes aren't what they used to be though. I didn't check the small print, you see. It's coming on the slow boat."

"Of course it is," Liz muttered, as she clenched her eyes together with a sigh.

Liz usually found Bob's quirks quite endearing, but when it came to his responsibility as her landlord, it was certainly not his forte.

"I heard you were staying with that farm boy," Bob said as he nudged her playfully in the ribs. "Aren't rushing to leave, are you?"

Liz blushed a deep crimson as Bob chuckled at his joke. Was it not possible to keep anything private in this town?

"We're sleeping in separate rooms," Liz said quickly. "I like my space, that's all."

"I'm not clueless when it comes to matters of the heart," he said with another deep chuckle. "Simon Greene is the man for you, Liz Jones!"

"Let me know when the new kitchen arrives," Liz said. "I'd quite like to get back to normal."

"You can have this month's rent for free," Bob

said with a wide grin. "And don't try to protest! It's the least I can do."

As soon as Liz heard this, the two weeks did not feel so long. She wondered if Bob even cared that she had burnt down the kitchen with her reckless attempt at baking.

"Well, I must dash," he said before rushing along the pavement, his bright yellow parka almost scraping the floor.

Liz walked back into the shop and continued setting up for the next instalment of her art club. Polly and Sylvia were the only two who had arrived so far. She wondered if they were going to be the only ones who did turn up. She could not imagine Lance showing his face, nor could she imagine Nancy turning up after their frosty interaction. She also would not be surprised if Debbie and Trevor decided to ditch art altogether.

"I think this is it," Liz said with an apologetic smile as Polly and Sylvia set up their workstations.

"We don't mind," Polly said, her squeaky Essex accent the ray of sunshine Liz needed. "We'll crank the radio up and have fun regardless."

Liz wished she had Polly's optimism. Years of

police work had jaded her view of the world. She was not sure if it could ever be repaired, especially when she kept finding herself in the middle of unofficial murder investigations. She retrieved a ram's head from behind the counter and placed it on the stool in the middle of the room. She had found the skull that morning when walking Paddy around the farm; it somehow described her current mood perfectly.

"How macabre!" Sylvia exclaimed as she riffled through her box of paints. "Well, I suppose we should get on with it."

At that very moment, Debbie walked in, followed closely by Lance, who looked like he had not slept a wink. Liz instantly noticed the stench of alcohol and that he was wearing the same clothes as last night. The bags under his eyes were so big, she wondered when he had last slept.

By the time Debbie and Lance had set up their easels, Trevor walked in to take his usual spot. Their arrivals surprised her, but she was even more surprised when Nancy completed the group.

Liz was happy to see Nancy, even if she was ten minutes late. Despite being scatter-brained, Liz could not remember a time Nancy had ever been late. She wondered if her friend was trying to make a statement, but she decided against looking too deeply into it.

Nancy took up her usual spot next to Lance. Liz noticed that her eyes were also red and puffy like Lance's, but she knew in her case it was from the lingering cold.

"How are you feeling?" Liz asked Nancy with a smile, hoping to defuse the tension lingering between them. "You're looking better."

"I'm almost through it," she said, a touch of sarcasm in her usually cheery voice. "I couldn't miss this."

Liz looked at the group, but no one else seemed to pick up on the strange tone of Nancy's voice. Liz tried to smile at her, but Nancy seemed to have decided she was going to avoid looking at Liz at all costs.

"I wouldn't wait for Catherine," Debbie announced. "She's probably at the salon having her hair dyed *exactly* like Katelyn's to complete the transformation."

The group looked uneasily at each other at the mention of Katelyn. Lance fidgeted in his seat, his eyes drifting up to Liz for a moment. His brows knitted together briefly before he turned his attention to his blank canvas. Did he even remember Liz's late-night visit?

"I thought we'd go for something a little different today," Liz announced as she motioned to the ram's head. "We haven't touched on animal anatomy yet, so I thought this was the perfect place to start."

"It's creepy," Polly squealed with a little bounce in her seat. "I love it."

"I do hope it died of natural causes," Debbie added. "I'd hate to paint a poor murdered soul."

Liz took her seat and began to sketch out the outline. Her lead encouraged the rest of the group to start their work. It almost felt as though nothing sinister had happened and they were an art club again. If it had not been for Nancy glaring at her from across the circle, Liz could have slipped into her special world. She had never wanted her classes to finish early, but today she could not wait to get away from Nancy's scrutinising gaze.

Feeling restless in front of her easel, she decided to walk around the circle. Polly had risen to the challenge and decided to paint the skull in pale pinks,

Sylvia trying to copy her again. Debbie's piece was abstract as usual, but it was less inspired than her usual work. Lance's work was drab and devoid of much colour. He had the proportions of the skull perfect, but it was the most literal interpretation she had seen from him. Trevor had once again started with a black canvas and was building up the shades in his usual gothic style. Liz came to Nancy's last, deciding not to linger for too long. Her proportions were completely off, and she had started with a garish shade of brown, but she seemed to be trying harder than ever. Liz wondered if she was trying to make a point.

Liz let another hour pass before announcing the end of the class. Everyone seemed to be in a rush to leave except for Debbie. Nancy was the first out of the door, followed closely by Lance and Trevor. Polly and Sylvia were the only ones to say goodbye to Liz. Debbie, on the other hand, remained in front of her painting, staring right through it.

"Debbie?" Liz whispered as she placed her hand on her shoulder. "Are you okay? We've finished."

Debbie blinked heavily, snapping back to reality. She stared up at Liz, tears immediately flowing from her eyes as her bottom lip wobbled out of control.

"He wants a divorce," she cried, cupping her face with her ring-covered hands. "Raphael is leaving me."

"I'm so sorry," Liz said, crouching to Debbie's side despite not having known she was married. "Come with me. There's a slice of cake with your name on it at Driftwood Café."

Debbie nodded through her sniffles. She wrapped herself up in a thick shawl before getting to her feet. Liz flicked off the lights, leaving behind their easels for clearing later.

Violet Lloyd, the kind owner of Driftwood Café, greeted them both with a warm smile as she wiped up a ketchup stain from a nearby table.

"Evening, ladies," Violet said as she pulled her little notebook and pencil from the front of her apron. "I'm afraid the kitchen is closed for the night, but we still have whatever cakes are on display."

"Can I have a coffee please?" Liz said as they sat at the table closest to the window. She glanced at the half a dozen cakes in the cabinet, her stomach rumbling a little. "And a vanilla slice, please."

"Uh-huh," Violet said, scribbling down the order after licking her pencil. "And for you, Debbie?"

"Can I have a green tea, and a slice of Victoria

sponge please?"

Violet finished scribbling down the order before stabbing the pad with her pencil. She turned and shuffled over to the counter, leaving the two women alone.

"We met in France six years ago," Debbie started as she stared out of the window at the purple sky. "I was on a spontaneous painting holiday on the south coast after packing a bag full of paints and canvasses. I went to paint, but I never expected to fall in love. Raphael walked over, and we instantly hit it off. He was tall, dark, handsome – the usual stereotype when it comes to beautiful men, but he was different. He saw me, somehow. The *real* me. I'd never been fortunate in love, but I fell hard and deep. We both did. I went home after two weeks, but he came with me, and he never left. We married almost immediately, and it was perfect."

Violet placed their cakes and drinks on their table before shuffling back to the kitchen.

"He's been cheating on me," Debbie continued. "I thought I could live with it, but he couldn't."

"He's an idiot then," Liz replied, sliding her hands across the table to grab Debbie's. "You're better than that."

"I don't blame him," Debbie said, frowning into her murky green tea. "I've always been ten years older than him, but it's never been more obvious than it is now. He's still as gorgeous as the day I met him, and I'm thirty pounds heavier and beginning to resemble an old shoe."

"You're still young," Liz said with a chuckle. "You're a couple of years younger than me, so what does that make me? An even older shoe?"

"You're gorgeous, Liz," Debbie said as she stared at her cake. "I don't even think I'm hungry."

Liz bit into her vanilla slice, custard flowing out of the sides. She caught it with her fingers before cramming it into her mouth. She was glad when Debbie copied.

"All I wanted was children," Debbie said through a mouthful of cake. "He said he was too young, and before I knew it, I was thirty-nine and childless."

"People have children later and later these days," Liz assured. "It's not like it used to be anymore. There are so many options. Simon's parents fostered for years, and then they adopted in their late fifties."

"But nothing is going as planned."

"Does it ever?"

"I dreamed of the perfect job, and the perfect husband at home with a couple of kids running around," Debbie said as she licked crumbs from her lips. "Instead, I struggle to get by selling my art online, and I haven't slept in the same bed as my husband for six months."

Liz could sympathise. She had been on her perfect life path until Lewis' murder. In those early days after the funeral, there had been times she had thought her life would never contain any happiness, but here she was.

"It's never too late for a fresh start," Liz assured her before sipping her hot coffee. "I had a completely different life before Scarlet Cove, and I wasn't particularly happy with it. I left it all behind to take a chance on happiness, and it worked. You can still do that."

"I'm not that brave," Debbie said, pushing forward a shaky smile. "I'm not like you, Liz. I always thought if I had my art, I'd be happy, but even that isn't working anymore. It's disappointing me at every turn. I'm getting worse and worse at it. Would you listen to me?" Debbie paused, letting out an unsettling laugh. "No wonder my nickname was Debbie Downer at college."

"Nicknames are silly."

"But it's true," Debbie said with a heavy sigh. "Nothing has ever gone right for me since then. I graduated, but hardly. My art was always too 'out there'. Katelyn graduated with honours. She stuck to the rules, and she was rewarded for it. Working at the gallery would have changed everything, and *she* got that job. We both applied for the position at the same time, and I didn't even get an interview. I would have made that gallery a place for everyone. We all deserve a chance."

"You're right," Liz agreed. "Our exhibition proved that, but it's not too late. Can you not talk to the people who own it? Catherine might not have the job on a permanent basis. They might be looking for a new lease of life."

"It's a faceless company," Debbie said with another heavy sigh. "Catherine wanted that job as desperately as I did. She might have bowed to Katelyn's every demand, but she's a ruthless woman. You saw that. She wouldn't give it up without a fight."

"So, fight," Liz whispered with a grin. "Don't give up on your dreams. You deserve better than a man who is going to cheat on you. Don't settle for second best, Debbie. Enough women do that every single day. Don't be one of them."

They finished their cakes in a comfortable silence as the dark purple sky faded to jet-black.

Liz paid for their drinks and cakes before they left Violet to close up the café. When Debbie hugged her goodbye, Liz hoped she had succeeded in cheering her up, if only a little. She had been where Debbie was, and she knew how easy it could be to continue falling down that slippery path.

Standing outside Driftwood Café after Debbie walked off, Liz fastened up her coat, ready to walk back to the farm. When she saw Christopher cutting across the market square, she changed direction and met him halfway.

"Good evening, Elizabeth," he said, out of breath. "I was hoping to catch you. I heard you were staying at the farm, but Simon's parents informed me that you hadn't returned from work yet."

"Art club," Liz said, hooking her thumb over her shoulder to her shop. "How are you doing?"

As she waited for Christopher to concoct his reply, she realised this was the first time she had seen him without his fiancée stuck to his side.

"Things are fine," Christopher answered in an unconvincing voice. "Lizzie and I were wondering if you and Simon would like to join us for dinner tomorrow evening."

Liz opened her mouth to reply, but no words came out. An invitation to dinner with Christopher's fiancée was the last thing she expected to hear.

"Oh," Liz said. "I would have to ask Simon."

"I want Lizzie to meet my friends," Christopher replied, not seeming to note Liz's reservations. "After all, she is going to be my wife very soon, and I want her to feel right at home."

"I'll have to ask -"

"*Brilliant!*" Christopher interjected, flashing his sparkling white teeth. "I'll see you tomorrow at eight."

Christopher turned on his heels and marched back the way he had come before Liz had a chance to say another word. An evening with Christopher and his new fiancée was not Liz's idea of fun. She was sure Simon would object, but Liz had heard hopefulness in Christopher's voice that she could not disappoint. Liz knew she needed to give Lizzie a chance for Christopher's sake.

Nine

At ten to eight the next evening, Liz and Simon found themselves standing outside Christopher's Victorian townhouse. Tucked away on the edge of Scarlet Cove, the beautiful four-story white house, which was as wide as it was tall, was nestled between a luxury spa and a bed and breakfast, the latter proudly boasting its five-star rating and '*NO VACANCIES*' sign.

"I've never been to this side of town before," Liz

muttered as she looked up at the gorgeous building in awe. "How the other half live, eh?"

"I'll take my farm any day of the week," Simon replied as he tugged at his cotton shirt collar. "I still can't believe you've convinced me it's a good idea to have dinner at Fishy Chris' house."

"It's good to make friends," Liz said, turning to look at the lighthouse as its golden beam washed the dark ocean. "They have a great view here."

"Best view at street level in the whole town," Simon said as he examined the wine they had picked up at the corner shop on the way to '*The Posh End*', as Sandra had referred to it. "How do I look?"

Liz dusted down the shoulders of the tweed jacket Simon had borrowed from his father before pecking him on the cheek.

"As handsome as the day I met you."

With her arm tucked around Simon's, they walked up the three immaculate steps to the front door, which was flanked by two ornate Romanesque columns. Liz reached out her hand to ring the doorbell, but Simon pulled her back at the last second.

"It's not too late to leave," Simon whispered with

a playful grin. "We can take this wine up to the castle and act like teenagers instead."

As tempting as the idea was, she pressed the doorbell anyway, much to Simon's disappointment. She looked down at the calf-length black dress she had retrieved from her flat and had dry-cleaned especially. Given a choice, she would have chosen a comfortable pair of jeans and a jumper, but she imagined Lizzie would be wearing something gorgeous.

Liz knew she could never compete with the Australian beauty, but the green-eyed monster buried deep within urged her to try. Simon's speechless reaction to her makeover after letting Polly Spragg blow-dry her hair and apply a little makeup had given her hope that she could at least raise one of Lizzie's eyebrows. She had asked herself why she cared so much, but her detective skills had yet to reach a conclusion.

The door burst open with a flurry of chaos. A golden Pomeranian darted through Christopher's legs, almost knocking him off his feet. Liz scooped up the miniature dog with one hand. She passed it back to Christopher through the gap as he fought to stop the other two yapping dogs from darting out.

"*Elizabeth*!" Christopher cried, his face red as white strands of his hair broke-free from their slicked back position. "You both came! Sorry about the dogs. They were Katelyn's, and I haven't decided what to do with them yet."

The three Pomeranians, two golden and one jet-black, sped down the hallway, ruffling the rug. Liz still could not wrap her head around the thought of Katelyn owning anything that she could describe as '*cute*'. If Liz was going to imagine Katelyn with a dog, the English Bull Terrier with its egg-shaped head and beady eyes came to mind.

"We wouldn't turn down an invitation to dinner," Liz said, pushing forward a smile. "Would we, Simon?"

"It's not like I had much choice."

Liz nudged him in the ribs while maintaining her smile. As Christopher kept the dogs at bay, Liz and Simon slipped through the gap in the door. She made sure to give Simon a '*play nice*' look as they did.

"We brought wine," Simon said, thrusting the bottle forward. "It's a pinot noir. The man in the shop said it would go well with fish."

"How thoughtful," Christopher said as he

examined the bottle at arm's length as though it was an explosive device. "We have an entire cellar full of wine, but I'm sure it will be *interesting* to try something from a shop."

"It all tastes the same to me!" Liz exclaimed with a laugh that sounded foreign to her ears. "You have a lovely home. Doesn't he, Simon?"

Simon grunted as he looked up at the glittering chandelier above them, a tight smile on his lips. If the hallway was anything to go by, Christopher's home was decorated just as she had expected. Classic dark wood furniture filled the space, each piece looking impossibly heavy. None of the furnishings shone lighter than dull beige, with dark greens and rich reds taking control. Aside from a modern telephone on the sideboard, Liz would not have been surprised if she had stepped through a portal into 1892.

"Katelyn picked out the art," Christopher said when he caught Liz looking at the dreary portraits on the walls. "Isn't it odd how someone can be here, and then they're gone?"

Liz rested her hand on Christopher's arm. He smiled his appreciation, but his momentary display of grief vanished. As though he had betrayed himself,

Christopher spun on his heels to lead them down the corridor. He straightened the rug with his shoe before turning into the sitting room, which was as extravagantly decorated as the hallway.

"These bloody dogs!" Lizzie yelled from her spot on the couch as the three dogs ran laps around her. "If I'd have known I was moving into a damn kennel, I would have stayed Down Under!"

"I'm sorry," Christopher replied like a berated child. "It shouldn't be too much longer."

"I bloody hope not!"

"What are you doing with them?" Liz asked, remembering how Christopher had almost given Paddy away to a shelter after his head fisher's murder had left the dog without a home. She hated to think what would have become of Paddy if she had not stepped in.

"I don't know," Christopher said meekly as he smiled at his fiancée. "I'll figure it out after I've finished planning the funeral."

The brief sadness returned to Christopher's eyes, but only fleetingly; no one else in the room seemed to even notice, except for Liz.

"I was saying to Christopher what a lovely home

this was," Liz said to Lizzie with a smile, shocked at how she suddenly sounded like her own mother did when she used to force small talk at the never-ending dinner parties through Liz's childhood. "It's very traditional."

"I think it's hideous," Lizzie exclaimed, her Australian accent growing shriller with every word. "If we're staying here, I'm redecorating as soon as we're back from the honeymoon. Something modern will brighten up this dark hole."

"If?" Liz echoed.

"We haven't decided where we're going to live yet," Christopher said, his stiff smile not shifting. "We've discussed staying here in Scarlet Cove, but Elisabeth is quite keen to return home."

"You bet I am," Lizzie said after tossing back the last mouthful of wine in the glass she had been cradling. "It's miserable here, and the people are so – so *British*! I'd jump on the first plane home tomorrow if I could."

Lizzie looked down into her empty wine glass with an exhausted-sounding huff. As Liz had expected, she looked stunning in a floor-length champagne chiffon dress that brought out the warmth of her tanned skin. Somehow, she appeared less refined than the other times Liz had seen her. Her hair was not quite done, and the flush in her cheeks told Liz she had been drinking wine for most of the evening.

"Is the food ready yet?" Lizzie cried, rolling her head back on the antique couch. "I could eat a dingo."

"Daniel, from the restaurant, is cooking for us tonight," Christopher explained, looking unsure of how to react to his intoxicated fiancée. "We'll be eating in the formal dining room tonight. I'll see how he's getting on, and while I'm there, I'll open this bottle of wine."

"I'll take a top up," Lizzie exclaimed, thrusting her glass into the air. "And I don't want a half-measure this time."

Christopher accepted the glass before hurrying off. Not only did he seem unsure of his soon-to-be wife, but he also seemed a little scared of her. Christopher had always struck Liz as confident, even if he did have a layer of vulnerability under his refined exterior. Since his return from Australia, he seemed different, and not for the better. Was it because of his sister's recent murder, or was there something else going on?

As Lizzie examined a chip in her nails instead of indulging in small talk with her dinner guests, Liz realised the dinner had not been Lizzie's idea. She felt foolish for going to such an effort to compete in a non-existent beauty pageant.

"Where in Australia are you from?" Simon asked, also noticing the stubborn silence. "I've never been, but I've heard it's lovely."

"Sydney," she snapped. "Best country in the world, if you ask me."

Simon shot the Australian a look that Liz knew read '*I didn't ask, but thanks for sharing*'. Luckily for the three of them, Christopher returned to let them know dinner was ready. Lizzie pulled herself off the couch before leading them through to the adjoining dining room. Her sickly sweet floral perfume tugged at the back of Liz's throat; it took all her energy not to cough.

"This is going to be a long evening," Simon whispered as he walked next to Liz, his hand resting on the small of her back. "Is it too late to take back the bottle of wine and make a run for it?"

"Don't tempt me," Liz replied before she realised

what she was saying. "Christopher needs friends right now, and he's hardly swimming in them, is he?"

"I wonder why?"

Simon's comment did not need further explanation, even for Liz. During her early days in Scarlet Cove, she had not taken the greatest liking to Christopher, but he had managed to change her opinion. When he stopped trying to win over her affections, she found that she quite enjoyed his company. He was socially awkward and often insensitive, but she knew that was a result of his boarding school upbringing. On paper, he was the last person she would find herself striking up a friendship with, but in reality, their differences made for interesting conversation.

The table was big enough to seat twenty, but only four places had been set under the glow of another chandelier. Liz and Simon took one side, while Lizzie and Christopher took the other. The three dogs hurried into the dining room and straight under the table. Fluffy fur rubbed against Liz's exposed ankles, making her giggle. Lizzie, who was sitting across from her, looked at her as though she was a piece of chewing gum she had found stuck to the bottom of her shoe.

Daniel Bishop, the owner of The Sea Platter restaurant on the coast, entered the room with a silver trolley. Even though Christopher had forced Daniel into bankruptcy so he could buy his restaurant, the two men were now business partners. After seeing the error of his ways, Christopher had agreed to go into partnership with Daniel by buying half the business. Daniel served as further proof to Liz that Christopher was not as bad as people believed.

"Cream of scarlet prawns and tomato with truffled seaweed and lobster coral," Daniel announced as he began serving the starter dishes. "Or in English, tomato and prawn soup with lobster chunks. Trust me when I say it tastes nicer than it sounds."

Daniel finished serving the bowls of soup before cracking open the bottle of wine Liz and Simon had brought. After pouring them all generous measures, he left them to enjoy their starter, which as he had assured them, was delicious. Lizzie and Christopher ate it as though it was a tin of *Heinz* soup from the cupboard, but Liz and Simon savoured every mouthful. Liz had never wondered what luxury soup tasted like, but she knew this was it.

"As soup goes, that might have been the nicest I've ever had," Simon said as he wiped some of the red sauce from his chin with a white napkin. "I can't say I've ever tried lobster before."

Lizzie arched a brow as though he had said he had never tasted something as trivial as an apple or bread. It had only taken one course for Liz to abandon all hope of warming to Lizzie for Christopher's sake. She disliked the woman, and she was not afraid to let that thought run through her mind. She reminded Liz of Katelyn, and that was enough for her to realise they were never going to forge a relationship.

The next course was low temperature cooked grouper on a tomato lagoon with marine plankton foam, which loosely translated into cooked grouper on a bed of tomato sauce with a green drizzle over the top. Like the first course, it was like nothing Liz had ever eaten before. She was glad that by the time they had all finished their main course, the conversation was flowing a little easier. Lizzie, however, had taken a vow of silence.

"I'm pleasantly surprised by this wine," Christopher said after swishing it around his mouth.

"It bears an uncanny resemblance to an excellent crate of pinot that I picked up from a winery in Burgundy when I visited France last summer. How much did this cost?"

"Six pounds and twenty pence," Simon announced without a shred of shame. "My mum likes this one for special occasions."

"Your mum has good taste," Christopher said, cocking his glass to Simon. "Good choice."

"I've never been able to taste the difference between most wines," Liz admitted. "It's either red, white, or rosé, and I usually go for whatever is on offer."

Christopher chuckled, but Lizzie shot Liz another disapproving look. Liz replied by sipping more of her wine before smiling across the table. She imagined Lizzie had grown up with a silver spoon in her mouth; it still seemed firmly crammed in there.

After a delicious dessert of rich chocolate mousse with a surprise brownie hidden at the bottom of the cup, Daniel came in to clear away the table. He filled up their glasses for the final time before wishing them all goodnight. When Liz glanced at the clock on the mantelpiece behind her, she was surprised that they had been there for almost two hours. Despite Lizzie's obvious discomfort in their presence, Liz was not having an awful time. From the relaxed look on Simon's face as he chatted to Christopher about his latest batch of cheese, neither was he.

When the conversation switched to Christopher's plans for his business in the coming year, Lizzie slipped away without excusing herself. It took Liz almost half an hour to realise that she had not returned, and she doubted she would.

"She gets headaches," Christopher explained when he caught Liz looking at the empty chair. "She's been suffering with them all day."

"How did you two meet?" Simon asked, now as interested in the unusual pairing as Liz was.

"It was during a gala dinner in Sydney that my parents were attending," he started, his eyes glazing over as he stared into the surface of his wine. "It was to raise money for a children's charity, so Katelyn and I went with our chequebooks to try and do some good. I was waiting for a drink at the bar when Elisabeth came over. We hit it off right away. She complimented my tuxedo and started asking about what I did for a living. She was the most beautiful woman in the room. I fell instantly in love with her."

It sounded more like infatuation than love, but Liz bit her tongue and sipped her wine, not wanting to burst his bubble.

"That was during my first week in Australia," Christopher explained. "We went on a formal date the next evening, and we continued to see each other every day after that. She was nice."

"Was?" Simon said, noticing the word along with Liz.

"*Is* nice," Christopher corrected himself with a firm blink. "When my parents encouraged me to propose, I thought they were being a little forward. I realised if she turned me down, I would return home at the end of the month with nothing gained. I bought a ring and picked a moment during a dinner that both our parents were attending. She said yes, and the rest is history. I ordered a new fleet of fishing boats, and there was a problem with production, so we came back to England. To be honest with you, I could have dealt with it over the phone, but Katelyn and I were glad of the excuse to come back. I can't help but think if we had stayed she – she would still be here, and this whole ordeal could have been avoided."

Christopher's eyes suddenly watered, and to Liz's surprise, he did not suppress them. The glittering tears rolled down his cheeks without fuss or noise. Liz remembered something he had once told her about boarding school boys being skilled at silently crying after years of practising in crowded dormitories. Without hesitation, Liz sprang up and ran around the long table. She crouched by his side, wrapping an arm around him. She looked across at Simon, hoping he would not be angry with her comforting '*Fishy Chris*', but he looked as concerned as she felt.

"It's okay to cry," she assured him. "It might help."

"Tears achieve nothing," he replied before dabbing them away with a napkin. "Enough. Death is as natural as life. We all have to go one way, it's unfortunate that someone else cut my sister's life short. Will you excuse me? I need to feed the dogs."

Christopher slipped from under her arm and out of the room.

"Poor guy," Simon said as he reached for his wine. "It's easy to forget he's real under that Victorian gentlemen character."

"It's not a character," Liz said, almost defensively. "That's who he is. He's as real as you and me. Imagine if your sister was murdered. Some people are more adept at hiding grief than others."

Liz flashed back to those first weeks back at work after Lewis' death. She had grown so tired of everyone asking her if she was okay, she had learned to hide her emotions; it did not mean she did not cry herself to sleep every night for months. That woman felt like someone she had once known in a dream, but the feeling could come flooding back in an instant when her mind wandered there. Simon seemed to notice her grief flash across her face because he stood up, his eyes filled with concern. Liz smiled, as she had when she was a detective; it was still easier to pretend it had never happened.

"Stay here," Simon said as he walked around the table. "I'm going to talk to him."

"Are you sure?" Liz said, swallowing the lump in her throat as she re-joined the present day.

"Sometimes these things mean more coming from another man," Simon said before kissing her on the cheek, his calloused hand cupping her cheek the way she loved. "Trust me on this one."

Liz did not argue. The reason Simon had been so easy to fall in love with was that he was always surprising her. She would think Simon was one thing, and he would show himself to be the complete opposite. He kept her on her toes, revealing his soul like a delicate flower blossoming ever so slowly over a long spring afternoon.

Liz finished off the last of her wine as she stared at a stern-looking portrait of a man above the fireplace. She wondered if he was a great ancestor of the Monroe family or another dreary piece Katelyn had picked. Looking down into her empty glass, she wondered how much wine she had enjoyed. It felt like only two, but then she remembered that Daniel had topped up her glass to the brim between each course, making it almost impossible to calculate how much alcohol she had consumed. Either way, the urge to use the bathroom overtook her.

Ditching the glass on the table, she hobbled towards the kitchen, stopping in her tracks when she saw Simon comforting Christopher as he sobbed on his shoulder. It warmed her heart too much to interrupt them for the sake of her bladder. Doubling back to the hallway, she peered up the long staircase, and then back into the sitting room.

"It's a bathroom," she mumbled to herself as she headed for the bottom of the stairs. "How hard can it be to find?"

She hurried up the staircase, hardly paying attention to the formal family pictures lining the wall. When she reached the landing, she was relieved to see the bathroom right ahead, its door open and inviting.

Minutes later, Liz was feeling a lot better. As she washed her hands, she stared at her reflection in the mirror and blinked, the alcohol sneaking up on her. As she dried her hands on a fluffy towel monogrammed with '*C.M*', she decided it was time to leave. She was sure after Christopher regained his composure and realised what he had done, he would not want his guests to stick around.

With a relieved bladder and clean hands, Liz left the bathroom. She made her way to the top of the staircase, but an Australian accent caught her attention from the next room. Through a small gap, she could see the back of Lizzie's curls, and a mobile phone pressed to her ear.

"I *hate* it here," Lizzie cried, not caring about her guests downstairs. "No! I don't care about the *arrangement* anymore. I thought I could do this, but I can't! I want to come home. Daddy! *Please*! You don't understand how awful it is here."

Lizzie turned around, locking eyes with Liz. Her lips stopped moving, and she closed the door, not without giving Liz one last stern look for the evening. Knowing she had heard more than enough, Liz hurried back downstairs, ready to share her eavesdropping with Christopher.

As she reached the hallway, the doorbell chimed, echoing in every corner. When Christopher did not rush to answer, she turned to the door, wondering who could be calling so late at night. Realising if she did not answer no one would, she hurried forward and opened the door.

"It's *freezing* out here!" an old woman with crispy white curls exclaimed as she dumped a bag in Liz's arms. "What took you so long?"

The woman marched into the house, a fur scarf around her neck and leather gloves on her hands. A short, plump man with a hunched back followed with a lumbering walk, his head of wispy yellow hair pointed at the ground.

"Terribly sorry about her," the man said in a

bumbling voice as he also dumped his bag in Liz's arms. "She's not herself when she travels."

Both of them shrugged off their coats before tossing them over the bags that they had forced on Liz. She looked down at them, wondering if she had transfigured into a hat stand.

"Are you going to *stand* there?" the woman snapped, her eyes wide as she stared through Liz. "*Where* is my son?"

"Be *nice*, Constance!"

"Oh, would you be quiet, Phillip?" she cried, turning her gaze to the little man. "The staff are paid to do as *we* please, and I *want* to see my son."

"I'm not '*staff*,'" Liz said as she let the bags and coats drop out of her arms and onto the wooden floorboards with a thud. "And if you're talking about Christopher, he's in the kitchen."

Constance, who could only be Christopher's mother, looked Liz up and down as though she had witnessed a dog standing on its hind legs and talking for the first time. Philip, the little old man, smiled his apologies at Liz as he shuffled past her to shut the front door. Both of them looked like they had stepped out of a high-class restaurant instead of an aeroplane.

Christopher must have heard, or at least sensed, his parents' arrival because he hurried into the hallway, a confused smile on his face, which was unable to disguise his puffy eyes.

"*Mother*!" he exclaimed. "*Father*! What are you doing here?"

"We're here for the funeral, of course," Constance said with a roll of her eyes. "Your sister couldn't have died in summer, could she? I'm frozen to my bare bones. She always was *difficult*."

"*Constance*!" Philip said through gritted teeth. "Enough of that!"

"Don't '*Constance*' me!" she snapped back. "I've had to sit for twenty-two hours in business class because *you* didn't book first."

"For the last time, they were fully booked," he replied with a roll of his eyes, letting Liz know he had said the same line twenty times an hour for the last twenty-two. "There was nothing I could do."

"There never is," Constance said through tight lips, spinning on the spot when Simon followed Christopher into the hallway. "Ah! *You*, there! Take our bags up to our room. We'll take the master with the sea view on the third floor."

"He's not staff, either," Liz said, folding her arms. "C'mon, Simon. We should go."

Constance spun and looked at Liz like the walking and talking dog had started juggling while balancing on a unicycle. Christopher scooped up their bags, flashing her an apologetic smile.

"Have you been crying, boy?" Constance asked, gripping Christopher's cheeks with one hand as he passed. "Your eyes are swollen."

"Allergies, mother," he lied before hurrying up the stairs. "Katelyn's dogs are here."

As though they knew they were needed, the three Pomeranians rushed into the room. Constance shrieked, and Philip fell over, only catching himself with the sideboard. Liz had to stifle her laughter as the jet-black Pomeranian jumped up at Constance, his nails plucking holes in her tights.

Leaving the dogs to terrorise Christopher's parents, Liz and Simon slipped out of the townhouse into the cool air. They stared out at the dark water for a moment as the lighthouse scanned for boats.

"Well, they're more despicable than I remembered," Simon announced as they walked down to the street. "I'm even more grateful for my own parents."

"I'm not surprised Christopher is like he is," Liz whispered as she looked back at the front door as they set off home. "In fact, I'm surprised he's not even worse. How was he in the kitchen?"

"Oh, you know," Simon replied, his eyes darting away from Liz. "The usual. We talked. You were right about him not being so bad, I've never seen it before. I don't think we're going to be best friends, but he's alright, I guess."

"I'm glad you think that," Liz said, clutching Simon's arm even tighter as they turned the corner, leaving '*The Posh End*' behind. "Because I overheard something, and I need your help stopping this wedding."

Ten

"You'd think at my age I'd know how to do my tie," Simon said as he looked down at the messy knot he had created. "Mum has usually intervened by now."

"Come here," Liz said with a chuckle, untying the knot to start again. "Cross, wrap, pull, and tug. There. Perfect, if I do say so myself. Give a man a fish, and he'll eat for a week."

"Teach a man to fish, and he'll create an empire

on the Scarlet Cove coastline, putting all the smaller companies out of business," Simon said with a smirk. "Where did you learn how to do that?"

"I was in the police for fifteen years, dear," Liz said, returning his smile. "They teach you on your first day."

"Really?"

"Can't get the badge without it," Liz said with a wink. "You look handsome in a suit."

Simon turned to the full-length mirror attached to the wardrobe in Liz's bedroom at the farm. He tugged at the tight collar before fastening the jacket.

"Give me wellingtons and a fleece any day," he said as he ruffled his waxed hair. "You look beautiful, though."

It was the day of Katelyn's funeral, and Liz had opted for the same black dress she had worn at the ill-fated dinner party. A black cardigan over her shoulders and a neat up-do switched up the look, taking it from glamorous to functional.

"Can we do a jigsaw?" Ellie asked, popping her head around the bedroom door. "Please, Liz."

"We're going to a funeral," Simon explained, the word making him uncomfortable. "But we'll be back later."

Liz knew Simon did not want to go to the funeral; he had been surprised when Christopher had asked him to cater the wake, and had not been able to say no.

"What's a funeral?" Ellie asked, pushing open the door and walking inside.

Simon and Liz shared awkward glances before Liz bent down to be level with Ellie. She had always been the one to work with children when on murder cases, mainly because her superior officers, who were usually all men, assumed she possessed the skill because she was a woman. Liz was not so sure, but she had done it enough times to know what she was doing.

"Have you ever had a pet?" Liz asked after clearing her throat. "A pet that isn't here anymore?

"Do you remember Goldie?" Simon interrupted. "And when you found him floating in his fish tank?"

Ellie nodded, her youthful eyes fixed on Liz.

"Well, Goldie went to heaven, and sometimes that happens to people too."

"But we flushed him down the toilet," Ellie said. "To be with the other fish in the sewer. That's what Dad said."

Liz looked uncomfortably up at Simon who could only offer a shrug.

"Not like Goldie then," Liz said, turning her attention back to Ellie. "How about the farm animals? Have any of them gone – Simon, help me out here."

"We send the old chickens to be made into chicken nuggets," Ellie exclaimed.

"Okay," Liz said. "I can work with that. When chickens get old and die, they become chicken nuggets, and when people die, they float up to heaven to live in the clouds. We have funerals to say goodbye to them. They're sort of like a party to celebrate a life."

"So, the opposite of a birthday party?" Ellie asked with a wrinkle in her nose. "Will I have one?"

"Not for a long, long, long time, kiddo," Simon said, ruffling her hair. "Most people get very, very old before they go to heaven."

Ellie did not seem too daunted by the prospect of death. Liz knew intelligent children like Ellie seemed to grasp the concept a lot better than others.

"Is it sad?" Ellie asked.

"It can be sad," Liz said, knowing honesty was the best policy. "But it can also be a happy time to remember that person."

"Will you be sad?" Ellie asked, looking deep into Liz's eyes. "I don't want you to be sad."

"I won't be sad," Liz replied. "I'm going to support a friend, and he will be sad. So, I will be there to give him a hug and a tissue if he needs one."

Ellie wrapped her arms around Liz's neck and squeezed tightly before letting go with a smile.

"Now you're all charged up with hugs," Ellie said. "I'll go and start the edges of the jigsaw. We'll finish it when you get back."

"You can count on that," Liz said with a wink before ruffling Ellie's hair.

Ellie turned around and skipped out of the room, leaving them alone once again.

"You handled that well," Simon said as Liz stood back up. "My heart dropped when she asked that question."

"Kids like adults who tell the truth," Liz said as she pulled her phone from her small black handbag. "We should set off. There's nothing worse than turning up late for a funeral."

"If anyone asks, you were getting charged up on hugs," Simon whispered with a grin before kissing her on the cheek. "Let's walk. I could do with the fresh air."

The walk to St. Andrews Church was a pleasant one. Despite the dark clouds on the horizon, the rain held off, and the February chill was warming up thanks to the impending start of March. Liz could not wait for spring to start; she needed the fresh season.

They arrived at the church fifteen minutes early, but the place was already packed out; Liz was not surprised. Funerals in Scarlet Cove seemed to be public events. It did not matter who the person was, they were always well attended. Over her police years, she had been to plenty of funerals where she could count the guests on one hand.

They walked into the grounds, smiling as they went. Liz spotted her art group standing in front of the church. She was surprised to see that Trevor was not there, and even more surprised to see that Catherine was. Debbie and Catherine seemed to be purposefully standing on opposite sides of the group, not that any of them were talking to each other. Liz set off towards the group, but when Nancy caught her eyes, she walked away.

"When are you going to make up?" Simon whispered, his arm tight around Liz's. "I'm stuck in the middle of you two."

"Soon," Liz said. "I promise."

Liz tagged onto the end of the group next to Debbie. She wanted to ask how things were with Raphael but decided to wait until later in the day when they could be alone. She looked along the line to Lance. From the distant gaze in his eyes, as he stared at the ground, Liz guessed he had already helped himself to some gin.

"Are you okay, Lance?" Liz whispered, hoping to catch his eye.

"I'm fine," he said without looking up. "Absolutely fine."

Debbie rested a hand on his shoulder, looking as though she was about to say something reassuring, but he walked off before she had her chance.

"Makes you wonder how long any of us have left," Debbie said when Lance was out of earshot before nodding at the row of houses opposite the church. "I live across the road, and I have to look at this graveyard every day. Any one of us could be here next."

"I guess," Simon said, a wrinkle in his brow. "Except Katelyn was murdered, so it's hardly an everyday occurrence, is it?"

Catherine fiddled with the collar of her blouse, her lips pursed tightly as she glanced at Debbie. Liz wondered if she was standing with them due to a lack of other options. Liz looked around the church grounds, noticing the detective who had interviewed her after finding Katelyn's body. He was nearing retirement age, but he looked completely out of his depth. From the way he was looking around the grounds as though he was in the middle of a bad dream, she could tell he was no closer to catching the murderer. It had always been a running joke in the city that the smaller towns could not handle the more serious cases because their detectives were old and fat from years of sitting behind desks investigating stolen bikes and noise complaints.

"She's here," Catherine said drily as she nodded towards the road. "Here we go."

Liz averted her gaze to the funeral cars making their way towards the church. Silence fell on the chattering crowd, and heads immediately bowed. The hearse pulled up first, the coffin inside devoid of the usual floral sentiments. There was a single wreath on the lid, but none of the usual displays of

'*DAUGHTER*' or '*SISTER*'.

The second, and last funeral car pulled up next. Christopher stepped out first with Lizzie by his side. She looked stylish in a simple black dress and pinned back hair, while Christopher looked like his usual self in a suit. Liz tried to remember if she had ever seen Christopher out of a suit, but the image did not present itself.

His parents were both dressed head to toe in black, a dramatic mesh veil covering half of Constance's crispy white hair. Philip's shirt was crinkled, and his tie was not quite tight around his collar. He looked as though he had attempted to oil down his wispy blonde hair, but it fluttered in the gentle breeze.

"Let's get this over and done with," Constance exclaimed through pursed lips. "The hysterics aren't good for my health."

With Christopher's help, five other suited men, who appeared to have been provided by the funeral home, pulled Katelyn's coffin out of the hearse. The sea of people parted, making a gap for Katelyn to make her way to her service. Her parents walked behind, their eyes on the ground, and Lizzie trailed after them, looking as though she was suppressing a yawn.

When Katelyn was inside, they began filtering into the church. Liz and Simon held back for a moment, as did Lance, who looked like he had not decided if he was going inside or not.

When Liz walked into the church, she was momentarily taken aback by the choice of flowers. Blood red roses surrounded a formal portrait of Katelyn in the middle of the centre aisle.

"I've never seen red roses at a funeral before," Liz whispered into Simon's ear as they took their seats at the back. "Bit unusual."

Simon nodded his agreement as he looked over the order of service, which was short considering the numbers in the church.

Constance and Philip were seated at the front, and neither of them showed a hint of emotion during the entire service. At one point, Liz thought Philip was crying, but he was holding in a sneeze, which he let out in the middle of the Lord's Prayer. Even Christopher, who was not frivolous with his emotions, looked melancholy. Lizzie, who looked around the church more than once to glare at Liz, looked bored. The funeral seemed nothing more than an inconvenience to her.

When it came to the rest of the town, there were a couple of sniffles, but everyone seemed to be attending out of habit rather than caring about Katelyn. Lance, who had lingered at the back for the whole service without sitting, did not look like he knew where he was.

After the curtains closed around Katelyn's coffin, her parents led the way out of the church, followed by Christopher and Lizzie. A short walk took them across the town to the gallery, where the wake was being held.

"It's a little eerie having the wake at the scene of her murder," Simon whispered to Liz as they walked into the gallery. "Even if it was where she worked."

"The thought has crossed my mind," Liz admitted.

After the gallery filled, which was even busier than the day of the exhibition, Simon left Liz to oversee the buffet. Liz looked across the room, catching Nancy's eyes. The two of them would usually have been glued to each other's side by now, but Nancy turned and joined in a conversation between Polly and Sylvia.

"Very mature," Liz whispered to herself, accepting a glass of champagne from a passing waiter.

Nothing of note happened until after the buffet was opened. All heads turned to the corner of the room when Lance almost knocked over a bust sculpture from its stand. Catherine shrieked as she hurried over, catching it against her chest before it teetered off the edge. Without apology, he stumbled off, sloshing white wine over the edge of his tilted glass.

Liz looked around the room, but no one seemed like they were about to intercept the drunken man. She wondered how many people had joined the dots between his recent drunken behaviour and his past with Katelyn. Unable to stand by and watch, Liz approached him, caution in her step when she remembered their last drunken interaction at his cottage.

"Perhaps you've had enough," Liz said with a smile as she steadied Lance. "I don't think the wine is helping, do you?"

"You again," Lance mumbled, spit running down his chin as he struggled to maintain eye contact through his flowing hair. "Why can't you leave me alone? Why can't you *all* leave me alone?"

Lance pushed Liz away before staggering out of the room, leaving a trail of white wine behind him. A couple of people shook their heads, but most seemed amused as they picked food from their buffet plates.

"Cheese nibble?" Simon offered, flashing a metal plate in front of Liz's face. "Don't take offence to Lance. He was like this when she dumped him, but he came out of it. He's a good guy underneath, but he can't handle his drink."

"I'm fine," she replied as she plucked an appetiser from the tray. "I've heard that excuse more times than I care to remember. Alcohol shouldn't be an excuse to act like a fool, and yet it usually is."

"What about grief?" Simon replied with a soft smile. "That sounds like a pretty good reason to me. Keep out of his way if you see him again, okay? There's nothing you can do to help him if he doesn't want to help himself."

Simon kissed her on the cheek before heading into the crowd with his cheese tray.

Seconds later, Katelyn's three little Pomeranians darted into the room, weaving in and out of people's legs.

"I locked them in the disabled bathroom," Christopher shouted as he tried to chase after them. "Who unlocked the door?"

"This is why you shouldn't have pets!" Constance cried as the black Pomeranian ran through her legs. "Horrible little creatures!"

Liz tossed back the champagne in the bottom of the flute, wondering how long it would be until she could slip out. Spending the rest of the afternoon putting together a jigsaw with Ellie was more appealing than the wake.

With the two golden Pomeranians tucked under his arms, Christopher hurried out of the room. Liz managed to grab the black one, which seemed to recognise her from the dinner party because it did not put up a fight. She followed Christopher to the spacious disabled bathroom.

"Thank you," he said as he locked the door. "I didn't know what to do with them. I couldn't leave them at home."

"How are you feeling?" Liz asked. "I know I keep asking that, but you aren't being –"

"*Christopher*!" a shrill voice called down the

corridor. "I need you."

Christopher gave Liz an apologetic look before hurrying off to Lizzie. She was standing in the doorway of the main gallery with her hands on her hips, and her eyes trained on Liz.

Liz was about to walk back to the main gallery to grab another glass of champagne when she heard raised voices coming from the office. She walked over to the door, the '*Catherine Ford – Gallery Manager*' sign looking oddly out of place. She pushed open the already ajar door, surprised to see the back of Trevor's head; he had been noticeably missing from the funeral.

"This is *not* a gallery matter," Catherine seethed, trying to keep her voice low. "I've already told you there is *nothing* I can do, Trevor. You can snoop around in here all you want, but you're not going to find anything!"

"I want my money back," Trevor replied, stepping towards Catherine with an outstretched finger. "Katelyn ran this place, and she sold me *fake* art. If that isn't a gallery matter, I don't know what is."

"*If* it was a gallery transaction then *maybe* I could

have done something about it," Catherine replied, not shrinking away from Trevor. "But, like I've told you several times, I've checked the accounts, and it wasn't!"

Liz edged closer, not wanting to miss a single word.

"You need to sort this," Trevor snapped, raising his voice and pushing his finger closer towards Catherine's face. "I know a lot of people who could make your life very difficult."

"Is that a threat?" she cried, recoiling from him. "Why don't I tell that to the police? I'm sure they'd love to hear all about this. Katelyn might have sold you fake paintings, but you bought them thinking they were *stolen.* Last time I checked, Trevor Swan, that is also *illegal.* Now, why don't you get that finger out of my face and get out of my office before I call them."

"You wouldn't," Trevor whispered darkly.

"Try me."

Liz stepped back from the door and hurried in the direction of the bathroom, slipping inside when she heard Trevor slamming the office door. As she washed her hands, she stared at herself in the mirror, adrenaline reddening her cheeks.

"You still have a knack for eavesdropping, Liz Jones," she whispered to herself with a chuckle.

After drying her hands on blue paper towels, Liz made her way back along the corridor, stopping once again at the office door. This time, it was wide open, the sound of rustling coming from under the desk. Liz stood on tiptoes, expecting to see Catherine, so she was shocked at what she did see.

"What are you doing?" Liz asked, startling Nancy.

Nancy immediately stopped digging through one of the drawers, a fistful of paper in her hand.

"Nothing," Nancy said as she stuffed the paper back. "It's none of your business."

"You're making a lot of noise doing nothing," Liz said with an arched brow. "Why don't we drop this? We're supposed to be friends, aren't we?"

"We were friends before you thought I murdered my boss."

"You're hardly helping your case, are you?" Liz nodded to the drawer as she crossed her arms. "I'll ask you again, and this time I want the truth, Nancy Turtle."

Nancy sighed as she straightened up. She fiddled with her glasses, unable to look Liz in the eyes.

"I was looking to see if Katelyn made a note of my termination," Nancy said, her expression softening. "She was particular about paperwork, so I thought she might have done it before – well, you know. Before she was killed and turned into a living art installation. Please, don't say anything."

They both looked at each other, and Liz felt a twinge of guilt about the way she had suspected Nancy. Despite that, her suspicion did not vanish. A quick reminder to look at the facts flashed through her mind.

"I won't tell anyone," Liz said. "But you need to leave this office now, and don't come back here."

Nancy opened her mouth to speak, but Liz was distracted when she heard a loud metal clatter. She ran out of the room and back into the main gallery, where Simon was lying on the floor. His tray and cheese were all around him, while the three Pomeranians hoovered up the mess they had caused. Liz helped Simon to his feet as his cheeks flushed with his obvious embarrassment.

"I'm fine," Simon said, forcing a laugh as he

brushed the crumbs from his clothes. "I should have looked where I was going."

"Who opened that door again?" Christopher cried as he scooped up two of the dogs.

Much to her obvious disdain, he passed one to Lizzie, who held it at arm's length like it was a mouldy piece of fruit. Despite being obvious troublemakers, Liz thought they were quite adorable, not that she could imagine having three of them.

"What a waste of good cheese," Simon said, rubbing his backside as he picked up the empty tray. "Where have you been, anyway? I've been looking for you."

"Unintentionally investigating," Liz said as she scooped a champagne flute off a passing waiter's tray. "Who knew funerals could be so eventful?"

Before Simon could ask anything else, Constance marched over to the buffet table and straight for the cheese section.

"Who hired these awful caterers?" Constance cried with revulsion after picking up a cheese nibble from one of the trays. "Dear Lord! They're *dreadful*!"

"Constance!" Philip started.

"Don't you '*Constance*' me, you little man!" she

snapped back before hitting her hand against her forehead. "I've had it up to *here* with your comments."

Simon blushed deeply at Constance's insult, but thankfully for Liz, he did not take the bait. Constance looked Simon and Liz up and down before marching out of the gallery once more.

Despite his wife's remarks, Phillip snatched up a cheese nibble. He tossed it into his mouth, and he seemed pleasantly surprised.

"Very good indeed," he said with a wag of his finger. "Pay my wife no mind."

With that, he hurried off after his wife, his lumbering, jaunty walk almost comical. He looked as though both legs were wooden and he was made of stuffing from neck to waist.

"Almost feel sorry for the fella," Simon said as he nodded to Christopher. "Imagine growing up with *them*. I better go to the back and see if there's any cheese left since I'm now a tray down."

After looking around the gallery for a familiar face, Liz was surprised when she did not spot anyone from her art club. She walked out into the hallway, relieved when she saw Debbie walking out of the bathroom wiping her hands on her black skirt. Debbie glanced at Lance at the same time Liz did. He was slumped against the door, his fists screwed up tightly. For a brief moment, Liz thought he was taking a standing nap before his fists pounded on the door.

"This was *her* office," he cried. "Not Catherine's. Would she jump in her grave as fast?"

Liz and Debbie both stepped towards the intoxicated man, but they kept a safe distance. Lance wrapped his hand around the handle, twisting it open. The door opened inwards, but he stumbled backwards, unable to sustain himself with the safety blanket of the door. Debbie caught him and rested him against the wall, which he slid down with little fuss.

Liz turned to close the door, but she noticed a pair of black heeled shoes on the floor next to the desk. What she saw next turned her blood to ice. On the office desk were two shoeless feet, solid and unmoving. Liz pushed open the door further. The feet belonged to Catherine, who like Katelyn, was laid on the desk, her arms flayed carelessly over the surface. Her face had been painted in the same fashion, but instead of a curtain tie, she had a letter opener sticking out of her neck.

"Call the police," she whispered over her shoulder to Debbie, whose ringed-hand was clamped over her mouth. "It's happened again."

Eleven

Liz wrapped her fingers around the blue and white crime scene tape as the flashing lights from the parked police cars blinded her. She stood on tiptoes, attempting to look into the gallery as the white-clad forensic team made their way inside.

"We should go," Simon said, pulling on Liz's arm. "You can't do anything."

"I should *be* in there," Liz said, on tiptoes again. "I could help."

"Retired," Simon reminded her. "Remember? You left that all behind."

Liz huffed and shook her head, but it was difficult to banish the feeling that she was right back on the job. She stepped back, merging with the spectators. She looked into the sea of hungry faces as the sun set behind them. She scanned the faces, but only spotted Polly and Sylvia from her art club.

"Where are they all?" Liz whispered. "Which one of them did it?"

"Let's go," Simon begged, grabbing her arm again. "You've given your statement. There's nothing you can gain from hanging around here."

"I just need to look around the crime scene," Liz muttered, almost to herself. "Why didn't I take my chance before the police got here?"

"Because you know better than to contaminate a crime scene. Please, Liz. We promised we'd babysit Ellie. Remember?"

The mention of Simon's little sister was what Liz needed to bring her out of her detective haze. She looked around the scene, catching the eyes of the leading detective. He looked like he could not see his toes, never mind see clues to solve a double homicide.

"You're right," Liz said to Simon with a smile. "Let's go."

Liz wrapped her hand around Simon's. She let him lead her away from the crime scene, even if her mind was still there. She no longer had a shred of doubt that someone in her art club was behind the murders.

"There's someone in that bush," Simon whispered, stopping them both as they passed the Fish and Anchor. "Is that Lance?"

Liz shone her phone screen in the direction of the bush. It was Lance, and he appeared to be fast asleep.

"We can't leave him here," Liz said as she tucked her phone back into her pocket. "Help me get him up."

With an arm each, they pulled Lance out of the shrubbery. He let out a mighty groan as his lids flickered, the stench of gin strong on his breath. They propped him up on his feet and wrapped his arms around their shoulders to keep him upright.

"Let's take him home," Simon suggested, nodding to the path that led up to the farm. "He's wasted."

"He's also a suspect," Liz confirmed, looking back

at the gallery. "We need to take him to the police."

"Look at him!" Simon cried with a forced laugh. "He's in no fit state to answer any questions. You know as well as I do that they'll throw him in a cell until he's sobered up. At least if he's at home, he can throw up in his own toilet. If they want to question him, they'll find him tomorrow."

Liz's jaw tightened, but she decided Simon was right. For a moment, she thought how wrong it was for a detective to allow a suspect to escape a crime scene until she remembered she was only a shop owner. If anything, she was surprised she was not the prime suspect owing to the fact she had been there when both bodies had been discovered.

"Okay," Liz said, pulling Lance's arm tighter around her neck. "But we check on him as soon as the sun rises and if the police haven't talked to him already, we drive him to the station."

"Deal."

Lance attempted to move his feet as they dragged him up the steep lane to the farm, but it barely made a difference. Despite being a slender man, he was pure muscle. When they dumped him on his couch after digging his keys out of his pocket, Liz let out a sigh of relief as she massaged her shoulder.

"I'm taking these," Simon said as he gathered up the half-full bottles of gin around the cottage. "He doesn't need any more of this stuff."

Liz looked over at Lance as Simon poured the bottles down the drain. In his semi-conscious state, with strands of hair over his handsome face, he looked innocent. She glanced at the door where he had smashed the gin bottle; there was still glass on the carpet.

"He's going to have a banging head tomorrow," Simon said as he wiped his gin-soaked fingers on his suit trousers. "Will he be alright?"

"He's a big boy," Liz replied as she stared at the demonic portrait of Katelyn on the easel. "No one forced him to get into this state."

After locking the door and posting the keys back through the letterbox, they walked back to the farmhouse. Sandra and John were already waiting on the doorstep, both of them dressed up to the nines. Sandra had opted for a simple blue blouse and black trouser combination, her usually wild hair neat and pretty. John was wearing a pale pink shirt with the tweed jacket Simon had borrowed for the dinner party; Liz had never seen either of them so dressed up.

"Told you they'd be here!" John announced with a nod as he hooked his thumbs into his belt holes. "You don't half panic, Sandra."

"You know what I'm like," she said with a wave of her hands as she pulled her cardigan tighter across her chest. "I thought we said half six?"

Liz looked at her watch, shocked to see that it was almost quarter past seven.

"There's been another murder," Simon explained, his hand tightening around Liz's. "Liz found the body."

"Again?" John boomed. "Blimey, kiddo! You have a nose for bodies, don't you? I'm not surprised you were in your previous line of work for so long."

"Who was it?" Sandra asked, her hand drifting up to her mouth. "You poor thing."

"Catherine Ford," Liz explained. "The new gallery manager. She was killed in the same way as Katelyn Monroe."

"A *serial* killer?" John exclaimed with a shake of his head. "What has this town come to? The world has gone mad, I tell you. First Brexit, and now *this*! We can't get a break on our fair isles, can we?"

"Most people consider three murders to be the threshold to become a serial killer," Liz said before even realising it. "But that's not what's important."

"Should we still go to bingo, John?" Sandra whispered as she hooked her arm around her husband's. "A woman has died."

"We didn't really know the poor lassie, did we, Sandra?" John said as he patted her arm. "Besides, it's big money tonight, and you've got your glad rags on."

"It has been a while since we went out," Sandra said with a distant nod. "Ellie's already in bed. Poor thing was exhausted after today's calving. They're coming out like bullets at the moment!"

With that, Sandra and John bundled into their old and rickety Land Rover. They waved as they reversed out of the farm before turning and heading into the town.

"Are you okay?" Simon asked before they walked inside. "This can't be easy for you."

"I've seen more bodies than you've had hot dinners," Liz assured him with a smile, even if the image of Catherine's painted face had yet to leave the forefront of her mind. "What I want right now is a hot bath and a glass of wine."

"Go and sit in front of the fire," Simon said as he took her coat off once they were in the toasty kitchen. "I've got it covered."

Simon kissed her on the cheek before heading into the back of the farmhouse. As the sound of running water drifted down from the bathroom, Liz pushed open Ellie's bedroom door. Washed in the pink glow of her nightlight, she was fast asleep in her bed, her covers down by her feet. Liz crept in and tucked her back in. Ellie rolled over, her mouth opening, but she remained asleep.

"Keep your innocence as long as you can, kid," Liz whispered as she brushed Ellie's hair out of her face. "Being an adult is tough."

Leaving the little girl to sleep, Liz settled in the armchair by the roaring fire in the cosy sitting room. She rested her head against the back of the chair and stared into the flames, her mind racing. How had she not seen another murder coming?

"Your bath is almost ready," Simon said, appearing from the shadows with a glass of white wine in his hands. "There's more where this came from."

"Thank you," she said as she accepted the glass. "What's going on, Simon? I can't seem to get my head around it all."

"If you *can't*, none of us stand a chance," he replied, perching on the chair arm. "Try and take your mind off it and come back to it fresh tomorrow morning. There's always a new day."

"Unless you're Catherine," Liz said after sipping her wine. "Or Katelyn. Perhaps it's my lot in life to be surrounded by death."

Lewis flashed through her mind for a moment; for the sake of not overloading her brain, she did not linger on the thought.

"I'm not going anywhere," he said as he looked down at her with his dimpled smile, his youthful face glowing in the reflection of the flames. "Go and have a bath. I've even put some of Ellie's bubble bath in there for you."

"Bubble bath?" Liz asked with an arched brow. "I can't say I've had that since I was about Ellie's age."

"You're never too old for bubbles," he replied with a wink. "Now go. That's an order, Liz Jones."

Leaving the warmth of the fire behind, Liz took herself and her wine into the bathroom. Like the rest of the farmhouse, it was without fuss or ceremony, its mismatched furniture purely functional. The freestanding white bathtub with gold feet, which was brimming to the top with bubbles, had been pushed up against the far wall. The toilet was olive green, the sink was pale pink, and the cream and brown tiles looked to be from the 1970s. Overgrown green plants filled the empty spaces in the huge room, reminding Liz of a garden centre.

She removed the funeral clothes before pulling out the pins that were holding up her hair. When she felt her bushy hair fall around her shoulders, she felt a little more like herself. She dipped a toe into the soapy water, the heat sending a pleasant shiver up her leg. Holding onto the gold handles, she lowered herself into the middle of the bubbles. After dunking her hair in the water, she sat upright in the water, her knees tucked close to her body, the fluffy bubbles acting like a blanket.

Her mind wandered to Catherine, and then to the art group. They had all been there, and they all had the opportunity to commit the crime. Debbie, Lance, Trevor, and Nancy had all been hanging around the office in the run-up to the second murder.

A soft knock on the door brought her from her thoughts.

"Is pasta okay for dinner?" Simon called through the door. "We don't have a lot in, but I can make a mean tomato sauce."

"That's fine," Liz said, running her wet hands down her face. "Come in for a minute."

Simon opened the door, popping his head around the edge. His eyes averted from her seated position in the bathtub, not that anything was on display thanks to the bubbles.

"I need a sounding board," Liz said, hugging her knees tighter to her body as she smiled at Simon. "I have so many thoughts racing around in my head, and I know they won't go until I say them aloud."

"And talking to yourself is out of the question," Simon said as he crept into the bathroom after closing the door behind him. "That would be weird."

Simon sat on the bath mat. He rested his arm on the edge of the tub, his eyes locked on hers. Instead of asking questions, he waited for Liz to speak.

"I know it was the art club," Liz started, her eyes glazing over. "They were all there, and they all had the opportunity and the motive."

"Who is your prime suspect?"

"Catherine was," Liz said with a harsh laugh. "I

thought she had killed Katelyn to claim her job for her own. Unless she painted her own face and stuck a letter opener in her own neck, she's out of the question."

"And the rest?"

"Well, there's Lance," Liz continued, breathing in the steam from the hot water rising around her. "He has unresolved issues when it comes to Katelyn. His love for her warped when she ended things. Turning to alcohol was a coping mechanism, and he's slipped right back into that. What if he's not drinking because Katelyn was murdered but because *he* murdered her?"

"And Catherine?"

"I haven't figured that out," Liz said, her brows knitting together. "But he was leaning against the door right before I found her. He was *there*, and you saw how drunk he was. What if he didn't realise what he was doing? What if there's seriously something wrong with his mental health? A split personality, or psychosis. He might not even realise he has it."

"I know him," Simon said with a shake of his head. "As you said, it's a coping mechanism for pain. He's just Lance. He's a good guy under it all."

"He threw a bottle at the door seconds after I

walked out of it," Liz said. "I didn't tell you because I didn't want you to say anything to him because quite frankly, I don't think he remembers doing it, which means I couldn't ask if he'd meant to hit me, or if he knew I'd already closed the door. Either way, it's hardly the actions of a rationally-thinking sane person, is it?"

"Well, no," Simon agreed with a shrug. "But if you take out the split personality or psychosis theory, he has no motive to kill Catherine. Katelyn, yes, but Catherine? They don't even know each other as far as I know."

"Exactly," Liz said. "As far as we know. There's a lot that goes on that we don't know about. A motive for murder could be right under our noses, and we could be missing it."

Simon thought about Liz's comment for a moment as his fingers danced across the surface of the bubbles.

"Who else?" Simon urged. "Lance isn't your only suspect."

"There's Debbie too," Liz said. "She's had a vendetta against Katelyn since her college years, but that doesn't explain why she would choose to kill her now of all times. And she wasn't Catherine's biggest fan, but again, why kill her then?"

"There could be more to the story there too."

"I know," Liz said. "But I can only use the facts in front of me. She's as much a suspect as Lance because she was there both times, but by that logic, you and I are suspects too."

"How exciting," Simon whispered with a wink. "I could be a wanted man and I wouldn't even know it."

Liz chuckled as he brushed her wet hair back. She slipped into the bubbles, lying back in the hot water.

"Let's not forget Trevor," Liz continued after the water had warmed her chilly shoulders. "Katelyn sold him those paintings, which is motive enough. I overheard Trevor threatening Catherine in the office not long before the murder. He was demanding the money back, but she claimed it wasn't a gallery matter. I believed her, but I also believed his threat too. If I've learned anything about Trevor, he's not a man to mince his words."

"Well, there you go!" Simon said. "If he threatened her, he did it. Why didn't you tell that to the police in your statement?"

"Because I have no proof," Liz said. "I didn't

record his threat, and they would only have my word for it. Trevor isn't going to admit the conversation, which will cast doubt on my accounts of everything else. They'll start to question other things I've said, and then they'll wonder if I'm to be trusted. I know how this game works. If they can't prove it, they won't use it, and then I could end up being the prime suspect for knowing too much."

Liz paused, wondering if she should share the next piece with Simon. Not because she did not think he would believe her, but because he would not want to admit how incriminating it looked.

"I saw Nancy in there too," Liz said. "Right after Trevor was in there. She was digging through the paperwork. She said she was looking for a record of her dismissal. I told her to leave the office, but then the dogs tripped you up, and I came running. I left her in there, and I don't know when she left."

Simon thought about the information for a moment, his jaw gritting.

"That doesn't look good," Simon admitted. "Do you think she -"

"Killed Katelyn and Catherine?" Liz jumped in so that Simon did not have to say it. "She's our friend.

You've known her for years, and I've known her for six months. I love her, but I can't ignore the facts. She has as much motive as the others. What if Catherine came in and disturbed her rummaging? What if Nancy did find the letter she was searching for? What if Catherine took the letter from her and read it, so Nancy repaid her by sticking a letter opener in her neck?"

Simon gulped hard, his eyes dropping to the floor. Liz took a moment to take a sip of her neglected wine. Her hopes that vocalising her thoughts would settle them had been in vain; they were racing louder than ever.

"Have you started cooking?" Liz asked, her nose wrinkling. "I can smell smoke."

"Not yet," Simon said as he stood up. "I can too."

Simon stood up with the support of the bathtub, leaving Liz behind in it. When she was alone, she pulled the plug, climbed out, and quickly towelled off. She climbed into her fluffy black dressing gown, which Simon had hung on the back of the door for her.

Knotting the tie around her waist, she checked in on Ellie, who was still sleeping soundly. Simon met her in the hallway, his brows low over his eyes.

"I checked the fireplace," he said. "Nothing wrong there. Sometimes the logs spit out onto the hearthrug, and a piece of fluff catches fire, but nothing."

They both walked into the kitchen together, where Paddy was sound asleep in his dog bed. Liz pushed her feet into Simon's wellington boots, which were two sizes too big for her. As they both headed to the front door, they heard the sound of tyres crunching on the gravel outside.

"Parents must be back early," Simon said as he glanced at the clock. "The smell is even stronger in here."

When they heard a deep cry escape Sandra's throat, they headed outside. It only took seconds for their eyes to dart down the lane to the bright orange flames.

"That's Lance's cottage!" John cried pointing to the flames as thick, dark smoke filled the night sky. "Do you know if he's home?"

Liz and Simon looked at each other, both of their mouths seeming to dry out at the same time.

"Mum, Liz, stay here with Ellie," Simon ordered.

"Dad, come with me."

"I'm not staying anywhere!" Liz said adamantly, stepping off the doorstep in the too big boots.

There was no time to argue, so they left Sandra on the doorstep as she called for the fire brigade and an ambulance. Simon and John sprinted down the lane, but Liz stayed close behind, clutching the front of her dressing gown. Somewhere along the way, the baggy boots sank into a muddy puddle and did not come back, leaving her to run barefoot down the lane.

"*Crikey*!" John cried, covering his face when they reached the blazing cottage. "Are you sure he's in there?"

"*We* put him in there," Simon cried as he shrugged off his suit jacket. "Dad, give me your shirt."

Without questioning his son, John shrugged off his tweed jacket before ripping open his shirt. He passed it to Simon, who wrapped it around his nose and mouth without a moment's hesitation.

"Simon!" Liz cried, grabbing his arm. "Don't be stupid! The fire brigade's on their way."

"The nearest station is ten miles away," he said through the cloth around his mouth. "This is my fault. It was my idea to put him in there like that."

Simon paused before kissing Liz firmly on the forehead. "I love you."

Liz knew she was screaming as Simon ran towards the blazing building, but she could not hear herself. She felt John's hands tighten around her arms, but it did not stop her thrashing against him. Somewhere in the distance, sirens blared out, but they were still miles away.

"Where is he?" Liz cried, looking back at John. "What has he done?"

The front window shattered, sending shards of glass flying towards them. They covered their faces, but the heat was indescribable; Liz's kitchen fire paled in comparison to the blaze in front of her.

"C'mon, Simon," John roared through gritted teeth. "Don't do this to us."

Liz knew the statistics surrounding fire, not that she could bring any of them to mind. All she could feel were the sands of time slipping away, every crucial second mattering.

When she was sure she could not take another second of the torture, a dark shadow emerged through the smoke. When Liz saw Simon dragging Lance along the floor, she let out a cry she had only heard leave her mouth once before.

Seconds later, the frame surrounding the door collapsed inwards. It sent up a cloud of dust and ash as the flames licked at every inch of the ancient cottage. Simon dragged Lance far enough away from the building for safety before he collapsed onto the ground, his face blackened from the smoke. Liz dropped to his side, her arms wrapping around him as he coughed until he could not cough anymore.

"The ambulance is here," John cried, the relief loud in his voice. "And I can see the fire engine too!"

Liz stared down at Lance, his head resting on Simon's knees. He looked as out of it as when they had left him, but this time he was not moving.

Seconds later, two uniformed paramedics rushed over. One of them tended to Lance, while the other dragged a reluctant Simon over to the ambulance. Liz stepped back, feeling completely useless as she stared at the burning building. One single thought controlled her mind, causing tears to tumble silently down her cheeks. She knew she had been close to losing another man she loved.

Twelve

Liz woke with a start the next morning. Nightmares of Simon being engulfed in flames had swarmed her mind all night, knocking her in and out of sleep at irregular intervals.

After calming her erratic breathing, she wiped the sleep from her eyes. She looked down at Simon, who was peacefully asleep next to her in his cottage, snoring and unaware. There was a slight rasp to his breaths, but nothing that would not clear up according to the doctor.

Smiling down at him, she pushed back the urge to brush his messy hair out of his face, not wanting to wake him. After last night, she was grateful to see another day with him, and she wanted to soak up as much of it as possible. She peeled the covers from herself as delicately as she could, careful not to disturb him.

She had been so exhausted from the stress of last night that she had fallen asleep in the jeans and shirt she had dressed in after showering off the mud in the farmhouse. She had been out like a light as soon as her head hit the pillow on Simon's bed. She scrabbled for her jumper and slid it over her body. Thanks to the clock ticking away above Simon's bed, she knew it was just past six in the morning. As she scratched her frizzy hair, she decided to head to the main cottage; she was awake now.

The morning air was dewy and cold, so she wrapped her arms around herself as she quickened her pace. She tiptoed through the vestibule and peeked her head around the corner hoping not to disturb the quiet house. She saw no one in the kitchen, and as silently as she could, she crept across the kitchen. She almost made it to the hallway before a head popped out of one of the rooms.

"Simon, is that you?" Sandra called. "*Ah*! Liz! An early bird like me, I see."

"I couldn't sleep," Liz said as she returned to the kitchen to sit on one of the mismatched chairs situated around the table. "Bad dreams."

"I'm not surprised after what you saw last night," Sandra said, her hand resting on the back of Liz's head like she was a little girl. "I only had my John's description, and even I was restless last night. I wouldn't trade my early mornings for anything though. When you live on a working farm, it's the one time of the day when I can go about my business uninterrupted!"

"What do you do?"

"Well, I catch up on the washing," Sandra said, almost a little disappointed by her admission. "But, *someone* has to do it, and I wouldn't trust my John with a spin cycle! He'd blow the thing up in days, I promise you. He can build a barn from scratch with a hammer, a box of nails, and scrap wood, but would he know which part of the tray the softener goes in? Would he heck! I've tried teaching him, but it's in one ear, out the other. That's men for you though, isn't it? Selective hearing." She filled up the kettle, heaving it onto the stove after lighting it with a match. "How about some coffee? I've never been one for the stuff myself, but I saw Simon had bought you some. Looks expensive too!"

"That would be great," Liz said, her body screaming out for caffeine.

When the kettle boiled, Sandra poured it into two cups, adding coffee to one and a tea bag to the other. She added a spoonful of sugar to her own tea but kept it black. Liz wrapped her hand around her mug when Sandra placed it in front of her, the warmth radiating through her.

"So, you stayed at Simon's last night?" Sandra asked raising a brow.

Liz felt her cheeks reddening, knowing that was more than enough to give her away. Sandra chuckled light-heartedly.

"You're more than old enough to do what you want," she said taking a sip of her tea. "I only offered you the spare room for your privacy. It was never against the rules for you to stay with Simon. Woman to woman, I'd kill for a night or two out of the master bedroom, but John would take offence. You think I'd learn to ignore his snoring after *this* many years of marriage, but it seems to get worse by the week."

Liz sipped her coffee, glad of the conversation. It was keeping her mind off the fire and what had almost happened to Simon.

"Forgive me for being nosy," Sandra started again. "And you don't have to tell me anything if you don't want to, but I have a feeling you have a past that you're not sharing with us. As I said, you don't have to say anything, but my woman's intuition goes off the radar whenever I look into those sparkling green eyes of yours. There's a story there."

Liz stared back at Sandra, her throat constricting as she tried to think of what to say. She tried to swallow the dry lump, but she could not manage to form any words. She had known this time would come, and she could not run or hide from her past forever, but she had hoped to have at least told Simon first.

"I'm prying, aren't I?" Sandra replied, a pained look on her face as she flapped her hands. "I'm sorry. The ramblings of a silly old farm woman!"

"No," Liz corrected, rubbing her fingers around

the brim of her coffee cup. "It's something I haven't told many people. In fact, I've only told Nancy so far."

"You can trust me, Liz," Sandra whispered, reaching out to grab her hands. "Whatever it is, I won't tell anyone. That's for you to do in your own time."

"I haven't told Simon yet."

"All I can tell you is how happy Simon is since he's met you. I've never seen him like this, and I know you're good for him. If you haven't told him, I trust there's a reason why."

Liz took a deep breath, readying herself to reveal the secret she had been holding on to since moving to Scarlet Cove.

"You know how I used to be a detective back in Manchester?" she said before pausing and looking down at the table. "I was – well – I was married."

"Oh," Sandra said, spitting her tea back into her cup, almost choking. "I wasn't expecting that. So, you divorced and moved down here?"

"Not *quite*," Liz said. "His name was Lewis."

"Was?"

"We worked together," Liz said before looking to

meet Sandra's imploring gaze. "He got in front of a bullet, and he didn't make it."

"I had no idea," Sandra said, taking her hands from Liz's and covering her mouth. "I'm so sorry. I should never have pried! That's an awful thing to have happened to you."

"I know he would want me to be happy," Liz said, wiping away a single tear that had managed to escape. "Lewis would have loved Simon. He loved everybody. He was really great, but that's part of the reason I haven't told Simon yet. I just don't want Simon thinking he's second best."

"He'll understand," Sandra replied after a long pause. "But I'm sure when you do decide to tell him it will be the *right* time."

Liz knew Sandra was probably right, but she had waited so long to tell him that it was getting harder every day. She always had a small thought in the back of her mind that he would not understand.

"Take it from me," Sandra said. "Tell him in your own time, but you *do* need to tell him. You can't build a relationship on secrets."

Liz nodded, knowing Sandra was right. She took a sip of her coffee, letting it warm her. They both sat in silence drinking their tea and coffee before John entered with a newspaper in his hand. He took his cap off and scratched his head as he stared at the front page before slapping the newspaper in the middle of the table.

"Would you read that?" he cried, rocking on his heels. "It's talking about Catherine's death. The police don't have *any* leads. None!"

"They always give the least amount of information they can unless it's crucial to finding the murderer," Liz murmured, taking the newspaper and noticing the date. "I need to go."

Leaving the paper behind, Liz hurried out of the kitchen. As soon as she stepped outside into the bitter morning air, she placed her hands on her knees and doubled over, feeling as though she was going to throw up. It was the three-year anniversary of Lewis' death; she felt sick to her stomach for having forgotten.

Things had been so busy the past week that the dates had flown by without Liz even noticing. She blinked in the crisp sunlight towards Simon's little cottage. She had a sudden urge to get as far away from the farm as she could.

After grabbing her jacket and scarf from the vestibule, she called to Paddy and clipped the lead onto his collar. She led him down the path, and away from the farm. Instead of heading into town, she walked along the top road and past Lance's burnt-out cottage. She could not bear to stop and look, so she carried on, her feet taking her to the Manor hotel.

Liz looked up at the beautiful hotel and its vast surroundings, the early morning fog giving it an eerie quality. Liz wrapped her arms around herself again and set off towards the grand doors with Paddy strolling lazily behind her.

The reception area was clear, and the receptionist was distracted with a phone call. If dogs were not allowed inside, no one was there to stop her. She walked through the sitting room, the paintings calling to her. She hoped if she stared at them for long enough they might unlock their secrets. To her surprise, Trevor was standing in front of the paintings, talking to an elderly couple. The hotel owner's eye bags were so large, Liz wondered if he had slept.

"I'll do you a great deal for the pair," he pleaded, a crazed look in his eye as he smiled deliriously at them. "I'll give them both to you for twenty thousand pounds. That's a *great* deal. Look at them! They're stunning paintings."

The couple smiled politely, despite looking scared of him. They both shook their heads and backed away a few steps.

"We heard they're fakes," the woman replied meekly. "Some of the other guests were talking at dinner last night."

"*Fakes*?" Trevor boomed, running his hand over his balding head. "Absolutely *preposterous*! I'm a respectable businessman! I'd never buy *or* sell fake paintings!"

"Sorry," the man said, leading the woman away. "We aren't interested."

"Fifteen thousand pounds?" he shouted after them. "*Ten thousand*?"

They hurried past Liz and out of the huge doors without looking back. Undeterred, Trevor marched past Liz and yanked on the doors.

"*Seven thousand*!" he cried. "You won't find a better deal!"

Paddy barked, knocking Trevor out of his trance. He looked straight at Liz and then marched past her as if he had not even noticed her presence. He looked at the pictures with such disgust that Liz would not have been surprised if he ripped them off the wall and threw them into the fireplace.

Tearing himself away from the fake art, he walked past Liz again and through a door next to the reception desk. Liz thought about leaving, but she wanted to speak to him. She approached the door with caution, opening it.

"Trevor?" she called into the room. "Can I talk to you?"

The owner looked up from his desk and grunted, looking unable to form a sentence. Liz took his grunt as an invitation, so she walked in with Paddy next to her side, shutting the door behind her.

"Take a seat," he said, motioning to a plush chair across the desk from where he was sitting. "Don't fancy buying some fake paintings, do you?"

His office was decorated similarly to the rest of the Manor. History oozed from the walls. It reminded her of Christopher's home, but it had a lightness to it that his townhouse lacked.

"If I had the money, I might have taken them off you," Liz said as Paddy settled at her feet. "Fake or not, they're still beautiful."

"Everyone knows they're fakes," he said as he sliced an envelope open with an ornate silver letter opener. "Someone must have overheard our conversation with the antique guy."

Liz stared at the letter opener as it glittered in his grasp in the early morning sun. An unnerving image of Catherine's lifeless body flashed through Liz's mind.

"I thought I'd be able to fob them off onto one of the guests," Trevor said, waving the letter opener around above him. "We have a lot of art lovers that come here. I might as well confess in the brochures that the paintings are fake. Not *one* person wants them."

Trevor tried to open another letter, but the opener snagged in the corner. He became frustrated quickly, tearing the metal knife through the letter, ripping it in half. It surprised her how quickly his rage could come and go.

"They look lovely where they are," Liz offered, trying to console him. "Keep them for yourself."

"I spent *one million pounds* on them," he snapped, forcing his fist down on the desk, the letter opener sparkling. "I'm sure even *your* detective skills can figure out that that's a *lot* of money."

"Enough to kill someone for?"

"I beg your pardon?" he cried, his face growing red as a vein bulged out of his neck. "You think I killed Katelyn and Catherine? I heard you used to be a *competent* detective, not a *foolish* one."

"I overheard the conversation you had with Catherine at the gallery," Liz announced, narrowing her eyes at him. "It wasn't exactly *civilised.* You threatened her."

Trevor stood up, the letter opener pointed in Liz's face before saying, "Why don't you keep your nose out of people's business?"

Liz stood up to Trevor's level. In the process, she accidentally stepped on Paddy's tail, causing him to yelp. In the few moments it took for her to look down at Paddy and back up at Trevor, he had closed the distance between them. He was so close she could see the little red veins in his bloodshot eyes. He raised the opener, holding it so that one slight mishap would cause it to plunge right into her skin.

They stood glaring at each other for what felt like an eternity before the door suddenly flew open. To

Liz's surprise and Trevor's obvious horror, two police officers ran into the room. They were followed by the plump, elderly detective on the Katelyn and Catherine case. Liz stepped to the side, pulling Paddy with her. Trevor opened his hand and dropped the letter opener onto the floor with a clatter.

"Trevor Swan?" the old detective said, his voice affected by a lifetime of cigarettes. "We are arresting you for the murders of Katelyn Monroe and Catherine Ford, you do not have to say anything, but it may harm your defence if you do not mention when questioned something which you later rely on in court. Anything you do say may be given in evidence. Do you understand?"

Liz watched in shock as the two officers restrained him before cuffing him against the desk. When he was secure, they led him away without a fight. The detective glanced at Liz for a moment, and then down at Paddy before also following. Liz held back, making sure not to get too close to the officers doing their jobs. When she reached the front of the hotel, she locked eyes with Trevor from the back of the police car; his face was devoid of any emotion. As she watched the car drive off, she had a feeling that something was incredibly wrong.

Feeling unsure about what she had witnessed or how the police had come to their conclusion that Trevor was guilty, she headed back to the farmhouse. If they had the right man, was that it? Was her investigation over? She looked down at Paddy as they walked back along the top road, unable to hide that she felt completely underwhelmed.

When she passed Lance's burnt-out shell of a cottage again, a figure standing amongst the rubble forced her to stop and look. It only took one step closer to see that it was Lance, standing in a hospital gown like a lost child. He spun around, and Liz averted her eyes when she noticed that his backside was not covered; he must have been freezing.

"Lance?" Liz called out. "What are you doing here?"

"I don't know," he mumbled, staring down at the hospital wristband still attached to him. "I was trying to fry an egg. I don't remember. It all feels like a dream, and then I woke up in the hospital."

"Let's get you back there," she said, stepping even closer. "You must be freezing."

Lance turned around, and the look in his eyes

made her double back.

"Leave me alone," he muttered before turning and walking barefoot through the pile of ash that used to be his home.

She waited until he disappeared over the hill before pulling out her phone to call the hospital to inform them where their wandering patient was. As she did, she stared through the smashed window into what used to be Lance's sitting room. Peeping out from underneath a fallen, charred beam, Katelyn's black eyes and red horns stared out at her.

Thirteen

Liz sat in the crowded Fish and Anchor, Simon by her side. The curious townspeople looked on in confusion at the sight of Christopher Monroe, who rarely stepped foot into the ordinary working-class pub. His beautiful Australian fiancée clung to his arm, a fake smile plastered on her face, raising even more eyebrows.

"What's Fishy Chris doin' in *here*?" someone whispered.

"And who is that *lovely* lady next to him?" another asked not so quietly. "I'll take you, love, if you get bored of eating fish every night."

Liz knew what everyone in town thought of Christopher, and his murdered sister would not change their opinions.

Christopher loosened his tie a little, looking uncomfortable as everyone stared at him. Lizzie looked unfazed and bored, which seemed to be her default expression. Christopher coughed to clear his throat. The room didn't quieten, so Lizzie tapped a fork against her champagne glass.

"As some of you may know," he started, pronouncing every syllable. "I came back from Australia with a beautiful fiancée and the love of my life."

Liz raised her eyebrow, but she kept her ears open.

"I have some wonderful news to share with you all," he said, his mouth stretching into something that resembled a smile without any emotion behind it. "Since my sister's murderer is now behind bars it seemed like the perfect time to announce that we plan to marry this Saturday, and you're all invited."

Christopher and Lizzie looked out into the sea of

shocked faces, waiting for a reaction that was not forthcoming. There were a few gasps as people exchanged awkward glances, but the pub remained otherwise silent. Liz could not stand the frown plastered on Christopher's face, so she started to clap and nudged Simon who followed suit. Eventually, the rest of the pub joined in, but Christopher's expression did not change much.

Lizzie rolled her eyes and walked towards the bar, leaving Christopher on his own. He continued to stare out at the sea of faces, unable to move. After an entire minute, he skulked off towards Lizzie, his head low to the ground like a wounded puppy.

"Poor guy," Simon whispered to Liz. "I bet he's been waiting his whole life to make that announcement, and nobody cares."

Liz glanced towards Christopher's parents as she sipped her wine. Constance was turning her nose up at everything as she wiped her hands with sanitiser. Philip, on the other hand, was deep into his second pint of Scarlet Cove Brew, most of the foam on his top lip.

"Haven't you told Fishy Chris what you overheard?" Simon asked after sipping his pint. "I thought you were adamant you were stopping the wedding?"

"I haven't had the chance," Liz replied. "Between the funeral, and Catherine's murder, and then Lance's fire, I've been a little busy."

"Well, you have until Saturday," Simon said. "Stay here, will you? I'm going to talk to that guy over there. I'm sure he owns a cheese shop up north."

Simon made his way across the pub, leaving Liz alone. She caught Nancy's gaze, who immediately started cackling at something Polly had said to her. Polly looked a little confused but joined in the laughter. Liz polished off her wine before turning to the packed bar for a top-up. She took a spot at the end, surprised to see Lizzie and Constance talking in the corner with their backs to everyone. Liz only had to move one step to the right to be able to overhear their whispers.

"I *can't* do this!" Lizzie moaned. "I thought I could, but I can't. I *hate* it here!"

"You don't have to live here *forever*," Constance said through gritted teeth. "We've been *through* this. You *only* need to have his child, and then you're free to do what you want. *One* child. Is that *so* difficult?"

"How long is that going to take?" she cried. "There's nothing to do here."

"Think about the *money*," Constance said, her hands gripping Lizzie's arms. "Imagine what you could do with it. Give it one year, and you'll be home pretending none of this ever happened. We have a *deal*, don't we?"

Lizzie mulled over Constance's words for a moment. She let out a long huff before turning around without saying a word. On her way, the Australian made sure to brush her shoulder hard against Liz's back.

Liz turned and looked over to Christopher, who was still on his own. She was unable to believe what she had heard, and her heart broke for him.

"What have you got yourself into?" she whispered.

"Huh?" grunted Shirley, the weathered landlady. "Same again, Liz?"

"Yes, please," she said with an awkward smile after turning back to the bar. "Make it a double this time."

With a large glass of wine in her hands, Liz made her way across the bar towards Christopher. She did not know how she was going to break the news she had just heard, but she knew she had to do it, and now.

"Christopher," Liz said in a hushed tone. "I need to talk to you. It's about –"

"It's time for us to go, Christopher," an Australian accent called from behind Liz, pushing past her to slide her arm through Christopher's. "Come on."

"But, Christopher, –" Liz implored.

"*Now*!" Lizzie shrieked, pulling him with her. "I hate it in this pub. It's so tacky."

Liz tried to chase after them, but Lizzie shot her such a look that it stopped her in her tracks. She knew as long as Christopher's little sidekick was stuck to his arm, she would not be able to get a word in. She was about to head back to Simon when she spotted Nancy again. Liz looked down into her wine before heading back to the bar to order another.

Now with two glasses of wine, she walked over to Nancy, hoping the drink would be a starting point to heal the rift between them now that Trevor was behind bars.

"Hi," Liz said sheepishly, handing Nancy one of

the glasses. "I got you a drink."

Polly looked at them both with a happy smile before scurrying off, much like Nancy did whenever Liz and Simon were alone.

"Thanks for the drink," Nancy said. "I'll pay you back for it. Did you hear about Trevor? The gossipers are going wild. They're all saying they knew it was him."

Liz thought about her reservations regarding Nancy, and she found it strange that Trevor's arrest was the first thing she decided to mention.

"I heard," Liz said. "I was there when it happened."

"I *always* thought it was him," Nancy said, a little too eagerly for Liz's liking. "There's something *strange* about him."

"You never said anything before."

"He's shifty!" Nancy said dramatically. "He gives me goosebumps. Don't you think he's weird?"

Liz did not know what to say. She had to agree that Trevor had been acting differently lately, but she thought it was more to do with the stress of the paintings than anything else. The police had arrested him, but she could not shake the feeling that there was more to the story.

"So, you think it was Trevor?" Liz asked, looking right into Nancy's eyes. "That killed Katelyn *and* Catherine?"

Nancy did not even blink before saying, "Well, who else could it be?"

"He wasn't the only one at the gallery both times," Liz said. "Was he?"

Nancy looked down at the wine, and then up at Liz. She fiddled with her glasses before placing the wine glass on top of the fruit machine next to them.

"You know, I thought that was a peace offering," Nancy said with a sad smile. "Turns out you *still* think it was me."

Nancy walked off before Liz could say anything else. She looked up at the wine, feeling foolish for thinking it could suddenly change things. It did not change the fact that Liz still suspected Nancy, even if Trevor was behind bars.

"We should go," Simon said, reappearing behind her to Liz's relief. "Mum texted to say dinner will be ready soon. It's her special casserole, and trust me when I say you don't want to miss it."

They walked out of the pub arm in arm, the bitter early evening air hitting them. Simon turned his collar up as they set off towards the lane leading up to the farm.

"I saw you and Nancy talking," he said. "From the way she walked off, I guess things aren't fixed?"

"I think I made things worse."

Liz wanted to air her doubts to Simon, even though she knew how he would react. It had felt like Nancy was trying to push her negative opinion of Trevor onto Liz as a way to prove her innocence. It only screamed of her possible guilt. She hated thinking of her friend in that way, but it was a classic manipulation tactic she had seen time and time again in interviews.

When they reached the bottom of the lane, they both stopped in their tracks, fear freezing them in place as a car hurtled towards them. Simon pushed Liz away, sending her tumbling over a low bush. She caught her balance in time to see Simon dive out of the way himself before the car veered past them.

The reckless car zoomed out of the lane and into the market square. With a crunch of metal, it crashed right into one of the stalls, the bonnet bending in on itself. After the bang stopped echoing around the square, Liz's ears began to ring.

"Are you okay?" Simon said as he helped her up.

"I am," Liz said as she dusted the leaves from her coat. "But I don't think they are."

They ran over to the car as smoke curled from under the bonnet. Liz stared through the window; Lance was behind the wheel. Blood trickled from a cut in his eyebrow, but he seemed to be alive. Even through the smoke, the smell of alcohol hit Liz in the face, almost causing her to gag.

"Does this guy have a death wish?" Simon cried, wafting the smoke from his face as he pulled his phone out to call for an ambulance. "Bloody hell, Lance! What do you think you're playing at?"

With Simon on the phone, Liz yanked on the door, and to her surprise, it swung back. She resisted the temptation to pull Lance out of the car, knowing that he should be left where he was until the ambulance arrived. She was glad he was wearing his seatbelt and that the airbag had activated. Liz had lost count of the number of times she had stared at his unconscious face recently.

"Can you hear me, Lance?" Liz called into the car. "You've been in an accident. An ambulance is on its way."

Lance opened his eyes long enough to stare up at

Liz like a child looking up at its mother.

"Katelyn?" he whispered before his eyes fluttered closed. "I – I'm sorry."

As sirens blared in the distance, she stared at Lance, her heart aching for him. She could not help but think his increased reckless behaviour thanks to the drinking was a symptom of something much darker than a broken heart.

"What were you thinking?" she whispered to him as paramedics rushed towards him for the second time that week.

Fourteen

Liz placed a vase in the centre of her shop before arranging various bouquets she had bought from the corner shop at the last minute. She had completely forgotten about the art club and was only reminded when Sylvia came by for some craft supplies earlier that afternoon. As she had finished arranging the colourful assortment of flowers in a way she liked, Bob hobbled into the shop in his usual yellow parka.

"I have some brilliant news for you," he said,

rubbing his hands together. "Your kitchen has finally arrived! I've got some men coming 'round to fit it this evening."

Liz was surprised that she felt a little down about the news. She had been looking forward to things getting back to normal, but she had enjoyed living at the farm. Seeing Simon every morning, if only at breakfast, had brightened her days.

"Thank you," Liz said, trying to smile. "That's great news."

"Loving it up at the farm?" Bob asked with a raised brow. "Simon better not steal my favourite tenant from me."

"Aren't I your only tenant?"

"Oh, yes," he said with a tap on his chin. "Well, you'd be my favourite even if you weren't. Next time, try and be a little more careful when you bake."

"Trust me when I say there *won't* be a next time."

Bob wished her luck with her painting class before tottering back out of the door. Polly and Sylvia quickly hurried in soon after Bob left, filling up the room.

"I love flowers," Polly exclaimed as she peeled off her bright pink coat and took her usual seat next to her grandmother. "Great choice, Liz."

Polly and Sylvia took their usual spots, but Liz was not sure if they should wait for anyone else. After Catherine's murder, Trevor's arrest, Lance's crash, and Nancy's behaviour, Liz was not surprised she had forgotten their meeting.

"Oh, dear," Polly whispered as she looked over at the door.

Lance pushed on the door, stitches in his eyebrow and his left arm in a sling. He limped in and dumped his bag on the ground before setting up without saying a word. Liz had visited him once at the hospital, but he had been completely out of it. Despite his injured exterior, Lance appeared sober, and he looked as though he had benefited from a decent night's sleep.

"Hi," Liz said, unsure of what else to say as she watched him set up his easel and paintbrushes. "Need some help?"

"I'm fine," he replied with a sheepish smile.

By the time Lance had finished setting up his easel, Debbie and Nancy had arrived together, both of them appearing to be in their own worlds. They sat down and set up without any fuss.

They all started to paint, the usual enthusiasm and excitement a thing of the past. Liz wondered why any of them had bothered to show up at all, but she could not help think that they were trying to prove something. She watched Lance and Nancy closely as they worked, hoping to see an admission of guilt in their eyes. As though they could both sense her watching, neither of them looked up.

"How's everyone getting on?" Liz asked, breaking the tense silence; only Polly and Sylvia bothered to reply.

Liz looked past the flowers and stared out of the window as the sun began to set. When she spotted Trevor walking past, his collar high over his face, she jumped up, knocking her stool back. Without a second thought, she ran out of her shop.

"Trevor?" Liz called after him.

He shot her a look over his shoulder before continuing. Liz jogged to catch up with him, so Trevor did the same. They almost reached the shore before he finally stopped and turned around.

"Why can't you leave me alone?" he cried. "Haven't you done enough already?"

"I haven't done anything."

"I *know* it was you who called the police!"

"Why would I do that?"

"You must have told them about me being in Katelyn – I mean – Catherine's office," Trevor cried, his eyes bulging. "They found my fingerprints all over the safe. I was only looking for my money. I didn't kill anyone!"

"Why did the police have your fingerprints on file?"

Trevor pursed his lips for a moment before casting his eyes over his shoulder to the sea. When he looked back at Liz, his look had softened slightly.

"I stole some cars when I was a kid," he admitted. "I didn't think they kept them for that long. It was never about the money. I enjoyed the thrill of it. It was stupid, and years ago."

"I still didn't call them."

"But you still thought I did it," he said, looking her up and down. "It's written all over your face. Why else did you come to my hotel to question me? You think some dodgy paintings are enough for me to murder two women."

Liz opened her mouth to reply, but no words came out. As she stared into Trevor's eyes, the hurt loud and clear in them, she believed for the first time that he was innocent.

"I don't think you did it," Liz said, lowering her voice. "But I'm getting closer to figuring out who did. It has *got* to be one of the people in the club."

"Is that supposed to make me feel better?" Trevor said. "I don't care anymore! My reputation is ruined. Accusations like that stick. Whatever happens next, my life is ruined."

Trevor turned on his heels and continued on his journey towards the coastline. Liz wanted to chase after him, but she knew there was nothing else she could say. She could not blame Trevor for the way he felt because she knew he was right. In small towns, accusations and false arrests were enough to smear a name if the real culprit was still at large.

Liz returned to her shop at the same time a large van pulled up outside. As if appearing out of nowhere, Bob bounced up to sign for the delivery before unlocking Liz's flat door, so they could carry up the twenty or so brown boxes.

"Easy does it!" he called out. "We've waited a long time for this."

Liz picked up her stool and resumed her place in

front of her easel, but she was unable to muster up the energy to even start painting. She stared at her blank canvas, never less inspired in her decades of painting. A quick look around the room told her that the group shared her mood, except for Polly, who had almost finished her painting.

"Let's call it a night," Liz announced. "I'm not feeling too great."

Lance and Nancy seemed the most relieved to leave early. They gathered up their things, their canvasses nothing more than a couple of pencil markings and faint brush strokes. Debbie had attempted her usual colour-explosion style, but even she seemed to lack the energy to finish.

When Liz was alone in the shop, she stared at the flowers as the last rays of the setting sun faded from the sky. Her mind was racing with dozens of questions, and yet she could not pin down a single concrete thought. She was sure she had the answer to figuring out the case, and yet it was clouded in a sea of noise.

She plucked her sketchpad out of her bag before flicking through the pages of scribbly notes she had made. She re-read over a couple of the pages, but nothing leaped out at her. She had written almost four pages dedicated to the fake paintings and Trevor's sudden shift in attitude. She tore them out and ripped them in two.

"You've lost your touch," Liz whispered to herself as she stuffed the pad back into her bag. "Perhaps it's time to give it up for real."

She finally stood up and packed away her equipment. When she finished, she picked up the flowers and placed them on the edge of the counter, not wanting them to go waste. As she inhaled the sweet scent of a rose, the shudder of an electric drill from her flat pierced through the silence, making her jump.

As the noise grew, she realised it was time to lock up and go up to the farmhouse for one last night. For the first night since Katelyn's murder, she decided she was not going to spend it obsessively reading over her notes.

After pulling on her coat and scarf, she flicked off the lights and walked over to the door. As she looked down into her handbag to find her keys, her eyes drifted to something on the floor. Squinting into the dark, she saw that it was a small sketchpad.

Liz scooped up the book and walked back to the counter. She sat on the stool in front of the till and switched on the small lamp. She turned the small sketchpad over in her hands to find a name, but there was not one. Aside from her own shop's sticker on the back, there were no other markings, and yet without even opening it, she could feel that every page was filled with art.

Liz flicked through the first couple of pages, which were full of simple sketches of landscapes and people's faces. She tried to figure out which member of her group the style belonged to, but nothing gave it away. All she could glean from the work was that it did not belong to Nancy or Sylvia. She flicked through the pages until the pencil scratchings turned to paintings. They were bright and abstract in style, but they were also vaguely painted. It struck her that they could belong to Lance or Debbie, but their styles were so similar, there was nothing to distinguish between them.

She turned another page, her heart jumping. She dropped the sketchpad onto the counter, an image that she had not been able to shake from her mind staring back at her. It was an exact replica of the messy painting that had been applied to Katelyn and Catherine's dead faces. Liz snapped the book shut, knowing that she had flicked through the mind of a killer.

The little bell rang out in the shop, knocking her from her thoughts. Lance walked into the dark shop, a small smile on his face. Liz's heart stopped as she glanced down at the sketchpad.

"I didn't know if you'd still be here," he said. "I've left something behind."

Liz stared at Lance, a lump growing in her throat. She looked down at the sketchpad again, the painting deep within its pages burned into her mind.

"Is it this?" she said, her voice small as she held up the sketchbook.

Lance took a step forward, squinting into the dark, but he shook his head.

"Not mine," he said with a shrug before turning and picking up his jacket from a basket of knitting wool with his sling-free arm. "Got it. Liz – I'm really sorry about what happened with the car."

"Don't mention it."

Lance looked as though he was going to push the topic, but he nodded before turning back to the door, the tiny bell signalling his exit. Liz looked down at the sketchpad again, her heart racing. She looked at her phone poking out of the top of her bag, wondering if she should call the police.

"You've just put your prints all over the thing," she whispered to herself. "You're an idiot, Liz Jones."

She stared at the book, trying to think what to do next, but the drilling and banging from upstairs was far too distracting.

"Liz?" a voice called into the dark. "You're still here."

Liz squinted into the dark as Debbie walked across the shop, the jangle of her bangles blending in with the noise coming from above. Debbie looked down at the sketchbook, and then back up at Liz, her face twisting into something Liz did not recognise. It was clear that both women knew exactly what the other was thinking.

Debbie moved so quickly that Liz did not even have time to react. She snatched up the sketchpad and ran for the door. Liz jumped up, knocking her chair over in the process. She ran around the corner, grabbing the back of Debbie's off-the-shoulder tunic as she reached the door. The fabric ripped in Liz's hand, knocking her back. It was enough to give Debbie her shot. With the force of a thousand men, she pushed Liz back, sending her towards the counter. Unable to stop herself, Liz tumbled back onto the counter. The edge of the wood struck the back of her skull, creating a noise in her head twice as loud as the drill upstairs.

Liz lay slumped against the desk for a moment, groaning as silvery stars crackled before her eyes. Through the haze, she saw the door fall back into its frame, leaving her alone in the spinning room.

Knowing she did not have much time, Liz rolled onto her knees, slapping her hand on the desk, glad when it met her handbag. She tugged it over the edge, its contents flying out. She picked up her phone, the bright screen piercing her eyes. She blinked hard as she felt something hot trickling down the back of her head.

Without a second thought, she called for the police first, and then an ambulance. After giving her address, the paramedic on the phone asked Liz how she was feeling. She tried to answer, but all she could think about was Debbie, who she had realised was a better liar than anyone she had ever met.

Fifteen

Liz stared at her new kitchen as she clipped her diamond studs into her ears. They were the pair she had worn on her wedding day, and she had only brought them out on similar occasions since. She hoped the diamonds would be a comfort to her as she watched one of her friends make a tremendous mistake.

"Admiring your new kitchen?" Simon asked after letting himself into the flat, already in his suit. "Have you settled back in okay?"

"I haven't been able to sleep," Liz said, her hand drifting up to the bump that still hurt on the back of her head. "Every time I close my eyes, I see Debbie hovering over me with her paintbrush."

It had been three days since Liz had confronted Debbie about her sketchpad, and three days since she had last been seen in town. Thankfully for Liz, the police had taken her seriously when she had run to them with her accusations. Thanks to unidentified fingerprints lifted at the crime scene, they had matched them to the prints covering Debbie's house.

"If she's got any sense in her, she'll be long gone by now," Simon said as he fiddled with his tie. "I bet she's on that same slow boat to China that brought your new kitchen in, which hardly looks any different, by the way."

Aside from a subtle change in colours, Bob Slinger had chosen an identical kitchen, with identical appliances. Liz did not mind; she did not intend on using it for anything other than microwaving for the time being.

"I have a feeling she's still hanging around," Liz whispered, turning to Simon, her eyes looking right through him. "Whenever I leave my flat, I can *feel* her watching me."

"You're paranoid."

"Possibly," Liz agreed. "But I befriended her. I trusted her. She opened up to me, and told me everything I needed to know to point the finger at her, and yet I let that cloud my judgement. I thought I was all about the hard facts, but apparently, I'm as human as the rest of you. I feel awful for even thinking that Nancy could have done this. I need to apologise to her, but she's been ignoring my calls, and she won't answer the door. I even sent a bunch of flowers to her door through one of those online things, but she sent them right back."

"Nancy needs time," Simon said as he pulled her into a hug. "She's sensitive. One time she didn't speak to me for a whole month because I made a joke about her fringe always looking a little too short."

"I like her fringe," Liz said as she pulled away. "I should have known better. I'm a fool."

"A loveable fool. She'll come around."

Liz hoped so. She turned to her sketchpad, which was sitting on the coffee table. She had pored over her notes a dozen times since Debbie had pushed her over. Every time she could not believe how extensive her notes on Nancy were, and how lacking her notes on Debbie were. The pieces were there in her scratchy pencil marks, waiting to be assembled. It made her wonder if she had retired at the right time.

Before they headed to St. Andrew's Church, Liz parted ways with Simon to walk across town to '*The Posh End*'. In the mess of the murders, Liz had let herself be side-tracked from what was important. She had been sitting on some information for far too long. It was only when she woke up that morning and realised that it was the wedding that she felt the urgency of the situation.

Standing outside Christopher's townhouse, Liz looked out at the choppy waves as dark clouds circled above. They could not have picked a worse day for a wedding. She spun around, feeling eyes burning into the back of her head. When she saw that she was completely alone, she hurried up the steps to the door and rang the doorbell.

"Elizabeth!" Christopher beamed with a shaky smile as he fiddled with his cufflinks. "What a surprise."

"Can I come in?" she asked, looking behind him to the dreary hallway. "It's important."

"Of course," he said, stepping to the side. "As it happens, I'm all alone, so the company would be quite nice. Mother and Father are with Elisabeth next door in the bed and breakfast, and my best man – well, I don't exactly have one. I did ask Daniel, but he wasn't too keen on the idea of the speeches, so I suppose I'll have to fill that role myself."

"Oh, Christopher," Liz whispered, resting a hand on his shoulder. "I'm so sorry."

"Don't be!" he cried so loudly it made her jump. "This is supposed to be the happiest day of my life."

"Supposed to be?"

"It *is* the happiest day of my life," he corrected himself. "I need to stop doing that. What is happening to my brain recently? All of those years of private education and it's already turning to soup." Christopher hurried into the sitting room where he took a seat on one of the antique couches. "Please, sit! I heard all about your scuffle with Debbie Wood. I must say I was quite surprised when the police informed me that she was the prime suspect in my sister's murder. I can't say I knew the woman much. I knew she jangled when she walked and always smelled of incense."

"It was quite a shock," Liz said, perching across from Christopher. "I haven't come to talk about that. There's something much more important that I need to tell you."

"Where are my manners?" he cried, clapping his hands together. "I haven't even told you how beautiful you look. Diamonds bring out the sparkle in your eyes. Can I get you a drink? How about a nice cup of tea, or maybe something stronger? I need something to settle my nerves. A little whisky should do the trick. I used to have a nanny I adored who would always put some on my gums when I –"

"*Christopher!*" Liz bellowed, forcing him back into his seat. "Please, listen to me."

Christopher nodded as he resumed his position in the corner of the couch. He stared at her like a naughty schoolboy who was not ready to receive his punishment for his bad behaviour. It broke Liz's heart to know that she was about to break his.

"It's about Lizzie," she started after a deep breath. "She's not all she seems."

"You mean to tell me she's not Australian?" he said with a loud chuckle. "She's exactly as she seems. In fact, I'd go as far as to say she's –"

"*Using* you," Liz jumped in. "She's using you, and your parents are using her. They're blackmailing her into marrying you, so she can have your baby to continue the Monroe bloodline."

Christopher's mouth opened and closed, but nothing more than a wretched groan escaped his lips.

"I know it might be hard to believe, but I wouldn't lie to you," Liz said, edging closer to him. "I overheard her on the phone to her father on the night of the dinner party. She was telling him she wanted to go home, and she didn't care about the money, and then I heard your mother during your wedding date announcement at the pub. She told her she was free to leave, but only after she had your baby."

"It's not," Christopher said.

"Not what?"

"Hard to believe."

"What do you mean?"

"I've known about it from the first night I met her," Christopher said with a sad smile. "I overheard a similar conversation between Elisabeth and Mother. Elisabeth's family came from money, but the recession hit them hard. Things had reached breaking point for them, and they went to my parents for a loan. That was before Christmas when Katelyn and I booked our tickets to visit Australia for the first time. I daresay they had been sitting on this plan since that day. I should have known it was too good to be true that the most beautiful woman at the gala would walk over to me."

"Oh, Christopher," Liz said, reaching out and grabbing his hands. "If you've known since then, why have you let it get this far?"

"Isn't it obvious?" he said, his eyes glazing over as he looked through Liz. "I wanted a shot at happiness like the rest of you."

Not only did Liz's heart break for Christopher, but it also shattered into a thousand tiny sharp shards. It was hard to hear, but on some level, she completely understood what he meant.

"You can't live a lie," Liz whispered, squeezing his hand hard. "You'll wake up every morning knowing it's not real."

"Isn't that better than waking up every morning alone?"

"No," Liz said without hesitation. "And I know that's not nice, but you deserve better than that. The right woman for you is out there, and she's not called

Elisabeth, with an '*s*' or a '*z*'."

Christopher chuckled, squeezing her hands back. He looked into her eyes for a moment before turning to look at the clock on the mantelpiece. His eyes popped out of his head, forcing him to jump up.

"You should go," he said, already walking towards the hallway. "I can't be late."

"Christopher –"

"Thanks for stopping by, Elizabeth," he said with a stiff smile as he held open the front door. "I appreciate knowing that I have someone in this town looking out for me."

Liz stepped over the threshold into the chilly air, unsure of what to say. When she turned back to protest further, the door had already closed in her face. She walked down the steps heavily and reluctantly, uncertain of what had happened. Before she could dwell on it any longer, she felt eyes burning holes in the back of her head again. She spun around, sure she had seen a shadow dart around the corner of the street. She hurried in her kitten heels to inspect, but there was no one there.

"Pull yourself together, Liz," she whispered to herself as she set off across town. "She probably *is* on the slow boat."

Liz met Simon outside St. Andrew's Church, which seemed to be as well attended as the funeral. He looked expectantly at her, but all she could offer was a shake of her head.

"What a fool!" he snapped under his breath. "Didn't he believe you?"

"Worse," Liz replied. "He's known from the start."

"And he's *still* going through with it?"

"That's what he said," Liz said with a heavy sigh as she looked across the street at Debbie's house. A police car had been parked outside since the night of her disappearing act. "Do you think she would be silly enough to try and get back in there?"

"The police must think so," Simon said as they walked arm in arm into the church grounds to join the rest of Scarlet Cove for the wedding. "Someone called my mum this morning claiming she's been spotted in Scotland. Violet from the café reckons she's been seen sleeping rough in London."

"*I* heard she jumped into the sea and was washed away with the tide," Lance whispered between them, making them both jump. "Who knows if she was trying to swim, or if she wanted to drown?"

Liz spun around. She was shocked to see that he looked sober and showered, and looking somewhat smart in his suit with his hair slicked back behind his ears.

"Good to see you up and about," Simon said with a heavy pat on his back. "How are you feeling?"

"Foggy," he said, his eyes locked on Liz. "I've heard I owe you an apology, or twenty."

"Forget it," Liz said with a shake of her head. "It's all forgotten."

"Which part?" Lance asked, his brows lifting up high. "The burning cottage, or almost running you over? I am sorry, though. I don't remember any of it, and I know that's not an excuse, but it's all I can offer."

"I get like that after too much Guinness," Simon said with an awkward laugh. "We all go off the rails sometimes."

"I've checked myself into a treatment facility," he said. "Moving in tomorrow for sixty days. It will give me time to figure out what I'm going to do next. I have nowhere to live, no car, and my reputation is in tatters. It's a good job my parents are dead, or else they'd be strangling me to death right now."

As though he realised what he had said, his eyes filled with sadness. Liz could not blame him for his grief making him do crazy things. For some people, insanity was an extra step in the process.

"Finding out that it was Debbie has given me some closure," Lance continued. "I've been off the gin long enough to remember that I stood no chance reconciling with Katelyn, dead or alive. Having her here always left it open in my mind, but it was a fantasy. She wanted me for my money, and I wouldn't wish that on my worst enemy."

With that, Lance patted them both on the back before moving to another group of people he likely owed apologies to. The parallels between Christopher and Katelyn's relationships suddenly struck Liz; they were two halves of the same piece.

Liz and Simon made their way into the church, taking the same pew as they had at the funeral. The chatter echoing around the room was almost unbearable, especially when it got to ten minutes past the starting time and neither bride nor groom was anywhere to be seen. As Liz fiddled with her watch, she hoped it stayed that way.

When Lizzie walked into the church, Philip on her arm in place of her real father, Liz's heart sank. Not only did she look beautiful in a figure-hugging mermaid dress with a long train and equally long veil, she also looked nervous. The quivering smile on her lips almost made her look human. When she noticed that her husband-to-be was not waiting for her at the front of the church, the quivering intensified.

"He must be stuck in traffic," Philip announced to the chattering crowd, much to his wife's obvious frustration. "He'll be here."

And Philip was right. Minutes later, Christopher walked into the church, a similar look on his face to that on Lizzie's. Constance breathed an audible sigh of relief, and Philip chuckled as though there was nothing untoward happening.

"Sorry," Christopher mumbled as he hurried down the aisle. "Traffic."

"Told you so!" Philip exclaimed. "Oh, don't give me that look, Constance. Today of *all* days!"

Christopher took his place at the front of the church, his eyes on the floor and not on his beautiful bride. When the priest, Father Dwyer, prompted Christopher to pull back his fiancée's veil, he did so with clumsy fingers. If he was happy to be going through with the sham wedding, he was not letting his face know.

The service went by slowly, and the usual talk of the roles of marriage mocked by what was happening in the place of worship. When it came to the part for onlookers to object, it took all Liz's strength, and Simon's hand on her knee, not to jump up and call out each one of them for their role in the deception.

"Now, this is the fun part, ladies and gentlemen," Father Dwyer announced jovially, not picking up on the obvious tension. "We've reached the part of the ceremony for Elisabeth and Christopher to say their vows. Are you both ready to repeat after me?"

They both nodded, neither of them looking ready.

"Then, as agreed, ladies first." Father Dwyer turned to Elisabeth, his smile wide. "Repeat after me, dear: *I,* and then say your name, *take you, Christopher Winston Monroe, to be my lawful husband.*"

"I, Elisabeth Daniella Wilson, take you, Christopher Winston Monroe to be my – to be my lawful husband."

"Very good," Father Dwyer chuckled. "*To have and to hold from this day forward.*"

"To have and to hold from this day forward."

"*For better, for worse.*"

"For better, for worse."

"*For richer, for poorer.*"

"For richer, for p-poorer."

"*In sickness and in health.*"

"In sickness and in health."

"*Until death us do part.*"

"Until d-death us do part," Elisabeth finished her voice suddenly tiny. "Is there anything else?"

"Now it's your fiancé's turn," Father Dwyer said with another chuckle. "You did very well."

Father Dwyer turned to Christopher to complete the vows. Liz was sure that Constance could taste blood from the ferocity with which she was biting her lip.

"This is the easier bit," Father Dwyer exclaimed. "You've already heard it all once, so simply repeat after me. *I,* and then say your name, *take you, Elisabeth Daniella Wilson, to be my lawful wife.*"

"I – I Christopher –,"

"Take you," Father Dwyer prompted.

"T-Take you."

Christopher paused and gulped hard before looking around the church, his eyes landing on Liz for a brief moment.

"I Christopher Winston Monroe, take you, Elisabeth Daniella Wilson to be my – to be my –"

"Dammit, boy!" Constance cried. "Stop stuttering. What's wrong with you?"

"Constance!" Philip mumbled, jerking his head to the church full of people. "Let them get on with it."

"Let's try this again," Father Dwyer said quietly to Christopher. "Nerves are normal. I've seen men twice your size pass out."

Christopher nodded and gulped again before looking at Lizzie.

"I, Christopher Winston Monroe," he started. "Do – *Do* –"

"Do take," he prompted again. "Do take, you –"

"But I *don't*," Christopher said suddenly, his eyes widening as he stared at Lizzie. "I'm sorry, but I don't. I thought I could do this, but I can't wake up every morning knowing that we'd be living a lie. I'm sorry, Mother."

With that, Christopher turned on his heels and hurried back down the aisle, gasps and whispering following him the whole way.

"Christopher!" Constance cried. "You get back here right now."

"Might I remind you, Mrs Monroe, that it is illegal to force someone to marry," Father Dwyer said, his tone shifting before turning to Lizzie. "I'm only sorry he waited until this moment to realise it was not what he wanted. Are you all right?"

Lizzie slid the veil from her golden ringlets before looking up at the high ceiling, a genuine smile on her face for the first time since Liz had met her. She looked like she was thanking her lucky stars.

"Keep your bloody money," she cried as she thrust the veil into Constance's hands. "I'm going home."

She hitched up her dress and ran down the aisle, a wider smile on her face than that of any woman jilted at the altar before.

"What money, Constance?" Philip cried. "What have you done now, you daft old woman?"

Sixteen

Liz and Simon left the church as the whispering erupted into full shouting as everyone speculated about what had happened. Liz had more important things to think about; she needed to find Christopher.

"Do you think he's gone home?" Simon asked when they were stood outside the church grounds. "Or to the harbour?"

Liz looked up and down the road, a twitch in the curtains in the top window of Debbie's house catching her attention. She squinted, almost sure her eyes were deceiving her again. When she saw a definite flutter in the fabric, her heart dropped to the pit of her stomach.

"Go and find Christopher," Liz said, gulping hard as she looked back at Simon. "I'll go and call Trevor and tell him he shouldn't expect a wedding party at the manor."

"Is that important right now?"

"Yes," Liz said, pushing Simon towards the road. "Go! Like you said before, sometimes it's better when men have heart to hearts."

Simon allowed himself to be pushed for a moment before standing his ground. He turned and looked down at Liz with a curious look. She flashed him a beaming smile, which she was sure looked more maniacal than reassuring, but it seemed to do the trick. Simon set off down into the heart of the town in search of Christopher.

Constance and Philip burst out of the church before jumping into one of the wedding cars and ordering the driver to set off. Liz wandered across the road to Debbie's house. She glanced into the police car, but the young officer's eyes were closed, his chin resting on his chest with his arms wrapped around himself.

"I'd have your job for that if you were my officer," she whispered as she unclipped the garden gate. "They don't make them like they used to."

She crept down the garden path, ignoring the front door, instead walking around the side of the small house. The back garden was wild and overgrown, with flowers of every colour jumping out for attention; it was like looking at one of Debbie's paintings.

Liz tried the kitchen door, but it was locked. She walked further along the house to the double glass doors in the dining room. To her relief, the left one slid open when she applied a little pressure on the handle. Holding her breath, she opened the door enough to slide through before closing it behind her. The colourfully decorated house was cast in darkness thanks to the closed curtains. There were no signs of any disruption, but Liz knew most people were more intelligent than to leave behind clues when they were sneaking about right under an officer's nose; Debbie had been doing it for weeks.

After checking the rooms downstairs, Liz headed

up the narrow staircase. The walls were lined with pictures of Debbie and Raphael from their wedding day to the present day. The further up she travelled, Debbie's smile remained the same as she grew older and heavier, but Raphael lost a little bit of the sparkle in his eyes, his handsome looks unchanging.

Using her powers of deduction, Liz figured out which room she had seen the curtain twitching. She pushed open the door, but she did not step in immediately. From her position in the dark hallway, she looked around the room as best she could, but it seemed empty.

"I hope I'm wrong about this," Liz whispered as she stepped into the room.

It was obviously Debbie's bedroom. One of her bright abstract paintings had been hung above the wooden sleigh bed. The covers were as colourful as the picture and piled in a messy heap on the bed. The rest of the walls were covered in smaller paintings, covering almost every space of the wall from the skirting board to the alcoves. Treading carefully, Liz walked towards the window. The curtains were closed and still, but she jostled them anyway, looking across the road as the church emptied.

"Why did you have to come?" a voice whispered behind her, forcing her to spin around.

Liz squinted into the dark, the ruffled curtains letting in a beam of light. A hooded figure stood on the other side of the bed, a large kitchen knife clamped in their hand. With their spare hand, they pulled down the hood. Liz squinted further, not instantly recognising the bald figure as Debbie.

"You shaved your head," Liz found herself saying as she spotted the familiar rings covering her fingers. "Must help you blend in."

"It was freeing," Debbie said, running her free hand across her prickly scalp. "I should have done it years ago. Why did you have to come here, Liz? I *like* you. This isn't going to be easy."

Liz looked down at the knife as it glittered in the light; she wished it had been the first time she had been in this position, but it was not. She looked around the room, hoping to find another door, but the only exit available was the door she had come through, and Debbie had that well and truly marked.

"You've been quite elusive," Liz said, her voice calm as she focussed on Debbie's face instead of the blade. "The police have been looking for you."

"I've been sleeping rough on the beach," Debbie said with a sniffle. "Wrapped up in a blanket, people thought I was a tramp. Woke up with coins at my feet more than once. Bodes well for my new life, don't you think?"

"New life?"

"France," Debbie said, her brows pinching together in the middle, a large chest at the foot of the bed commanding her attention for a moment. "I was never happier than those early days with Raphael. I can start a new life there. I can sell my paintings on the street and fall in love again. They don't call me Debbie Downer anymore."

Liz decided not to tell Debbie she would not get past the border with her passport. With the police looking for her, any chance of a new life off the streets would be almost impossible without a friend in the business of fake documentation.

"That sounds nice," Liz said, eager not to annoy her captor. "They'll probably have nicer weather than Scarlet Cove."

Debbie laughed, and the knife dropped for a moment; she seemed to forget what had happened. When she remembered moments later, she lifted the knife up again before taking a step toward Liz, making her escape path even narrower.

"Why did you do it, Debbie?" Liz asked, genuinely curious. "There were other ways."

"Were there?" she cried, the knife shaking in her hand. "Katelyn had *everything* I wanted. She had the job I wanted, and the talent I wanted, and she rubbed it in my face every chance she got. '*Debbie Downer should fall down and not get back up*'. That's what she used to say to me at college. She turned everyone against me. They all used to say it. I did fall, but I got back up, and I'm stronger than ever. The thought of killing Katelyn had been a constant one since then. It was quieter when I was happy with Raphael, but it only grew stronger. When she ruined my chance – my *one* shot to be seen the way I *should* be, I knew I had to do it. I didn't hesitate to pull that curtain tie around her neck. She *barely* put up a fight. It shows how *weak* she was underneath it all. Who's down now? She's nothing more than a box of ashes sitting on someone's mantelpiece, and even that's too good for her. *I* turned her into art – she was my best piece. Ironic, don't you think? She wouldn't display my art, so she *became* it."

Debbie laughed to herself, like a woman who had been told a childish joke; Liz realised she was not a sane woman.

"And Catherine?" Liz asked, eager to know everything now that the truth was rolling off her tongue. "I know she wouldn't display your work, but you didn't have a vendetta against her."

"I didn't plan to kill her," Debbie said. "But I'm glad I did. I thought maybe the funeral would have changed her mind. Seeing Katelyn's coffin seemed to soften her a little. I thought she might change her mind and agree to put my work up. She wouldn't. In fact, she was even worse. When she told me – when she told me that it was Katelyn who Raphael had been cheating on me with, I snapped. I picked up the letter opener, and I stabbed her. She begged for help, but she died pretty quickly. It was lucky there was a sample box of new paints on the desk so I could create another *real* work of art. Canvasses could never compare, but I suppose I'll have to adjust."

Liz heard a creak on the staircase, but Debbie did not seem to notice it. Liz put it down to the house settling until she heard it again.

"Why did you come back here if you're so set on

your new life?" Liz asked, keen to keep Debbie talking; if she was talking, she was not stabbing. "You've dodged the police for this long. You could have slipped away, and no one would have noticed."

"Because I'm a *fool*!" Debbie shrieked, her eyes as wide and white as the moon. "I knew everyone would be occupied by the wedding. My romantic side has always been my downfall. I came to say goodbye."

"To the house?"

"No," Debbie said, her eyes dropping to the floor. "To Raphael."

Liz heard another creak outside the door. She held her breath, knowing it was now or never. As she caught the door opening out of the corner of her eye, Debbie did too. Liz took her chance and picked up the messy duvet to toss it over Debbie. It was long enough for Liz to dart over the soft mattress and behind the officer.

"*Get on the ground*!" the officer cried before being followed in by two others. "*Get on the ground, now*!"

The duvet fell to the floor in a heap. When the officer ripped it off, Debbie had the knife to her neck as she sobbed, but she could not do it. The blade fell from her hand and onto the floorboards with a heavy thud. She was face down on the ground and cuffed immediately.

After they escorted Debbie out of her house, Simon darted up the stairs, his face sweaty and full of fear. When he saw Liz, he grabbed hold of her like they had not seen each other in months.

"I'm such an idiot," Simon said as he held her tight. "And you're a bad liar. I got as far as the pier before I turned back. When I saw you twitching the curtain of Debbie's house, I realised what you were doing."

"I'm fine," Liz said with a relieved smile. "I'm trained for this. She's been caught, that's all that matters."

"It's finally over," Simon said, holding her at arm's length. "Please promise you're going to hang up your detective shoes this time for real?"

"I will after it is really over," Liz said, nodding to the young officer she had seen asleep outside the house. "You there. What's your name?"

"Police Constable Brady," the young man mumbled. "David Brady, ma'am."

"You realise falling asleep on the job is enough to

have your stripes taken off you?" Liz demanded, the superior tone a natural one to her. "What would you have done if I, a stupid member of the public, had been murdered in here after I easily walked in because you were taking a nap on the job?"

"I'm sorry, ma'am," he said, his eyes on the carpet. "I argued with my girlfriend last night, ma'am. I didn't get much sleep, ma'am."

"You're lucky I'm a *retired* detective," Liz said more softly. "I won't tell anyone, but I want you to do something for me first."

The young officer nodded before following Liz back into the bedroom. She tossed the duvet onto the bed, walked over to the window, and pulled back the curtains, casting the colourful room in the grey afternoon light.

"Bust open the padlock on that chest," Liz said, pointing to the wooden box at the bottom of the bed. "Debbie seemed quite interested in it."

"But –"

"Do it, kiddo," Simon said, clapping him on the shoulder. "I've learned it's better not to argue."

PC Brady looked between them with red cheeks before pulling out his baton. With the solid butt of it, he beat the metal padlock until it burst off the chest. When he went to open it, Liz stepped in and took over. She pulled it open, and for one of the few times in her life, she wished she had been wrong after all.

"*Oh*!" PC Brady cried, his hand over his mouth as he stared down into the chest, where a man lay in the foetal position covered in a white chalky substance. "What is that?"

"I think you mean '*who*'," Simon corrected him.

"Raphael," Liz said, her hand also over her mouth. "Debbie's cheating husband. And judging by the looks of him, I'd say he's been locked up in there for at least a month, although it's hard to say with all the lime powder in there."

"Lime powder?" Simon echoed. "We used that on the chickens when we had a load die during that hot summer a couple of years ago."

"Stops the smell of decay," Liz said as she walked over to the window to push it open. "Although not entirely. Slows down the rate of decay by sucking the moisture and bacteria out of the body. Let's get out of here. It's become an active crime scene. PC Brady, call this in. I'll let you claim this one. Tell them you noticed the smell and don't mention the padlock."

Leaving the young officer behind, Liz and Simon set off out of the house and into the bright daylight. They reached the street in time to see Debbie being driven away in the back of a car, which was surrounded by everyone from the church.

"They're going to talk about this day for decades," Simon said with a shake of his head. "I'm sure Scarlet Cove wasn't this eventful before you moved here."

"Maybe I should go back to where I came from?" Liz asked, shielding her eyes from the sun as it finally broke through the dark clouds. "I seem to be a bad omen."

"But you're my bad omen," Simon said, pulling Liz into his chest. "You're not going anywhere, Liz Jones. You're as much a part of Scarlet Cove as I am."

Seventeen

When Liz announced to her art group that their current meeting would be their last, the three remaining members did not seem too surprised. In fact, Trevor and Sylvia seemed relieved, and it was only Polly who seemed upset that she would not get to paint every week. Liz assured her that they could paint together any time she wanted, which perked her up a little.

After they packed up their easels for the final time, Liz was glad to reclaim her shop for herself once again, even if she was sad that the group had failed. It had, after all, been one of Nancy's better ideas, but its execution had been more murderous than Liz had expected.

The trio left, leaving Liz to clear up alone. Before she flicked off the lights, a suited figure stepped into the shop, frightening her.

"*Christopher*!" Liz exclaimed with a laugh as her heart pounded in her chest. "You scared me."

"Sorry," he said with a meek smile. "I've been waiting outside for the meeting to finish. I wanted to get you alone to say thank you."

"For ruining your wedding?"

"Exactly," he said with a nod and a wink. "Lizzie and my parents are currently somewhere over Asia as they fly back to Sydney. When I actually talked to Lizzie – the *real* Lizzie – I could almost understand. Her father has been putting pressure on her for years to marry to save the family, so when this opportunity fell into her lap, she couldn't pass it up. She even apologised, which was nice to hear."

"And your parents?"

"Father said goodbye," Christopher said, his smile turning down at the corners. "I doubt Mother will ever speak to me again, which means two fewer phone calls a year. How will I cope without being asked '*are you married yet?*' on my birthday and at Christmas?"

"Sounds familiar," Liz said as she leaned against the counter. "Although mine ask 'are you still painting?', and they're not asking because they want something to hang in their living room."

"If I had a drink, I'd toast it to bad parents."

Liz picked up her dirty pot of paint water, tipping it to Christopher.

"To bad parents," she said with a grin. "And to new beginnings. We get them every day, and yet we don't even realise it."

"You're right there," Christopher said. "Since we're starting afresh, I suppose I should clear up one last mystery for you. It was I who put Katelyn in touch with the dealers about the fake Murphy Jones paintings, although I didn't know they were fake, I thought they were stolen."

"Of course."

"An old woman called Dot stole the painting from the coffee shop in Peridale after it closed, and then a young lad stole it from her, probably hoping to sell it for a few pounds. His father passed it onto the police, but it never made it to the station because the officer's brother happened to be an art dealer. It passed around the country and got coupled up with the second painting along the way until an old fishing contact of mine asked if I wanted to take some stolen Murphy Jones' off his hands. I had to research the internet for the artist's name, but when I saw how much his last piece sold at auction for, I put the dealer in touch with Katelyn. I *thought* I was doing her a favour. I don't know how I could have lived with myself if those paintings *had* been the reason for her murder, but at least that would have made sense. Do you happen to know what Trevor will do with the paintings?"

"His conscience got the better of him, and he destroyed them," Liz said. "It's never nice to see art die like that, but they'd caused enough trouble, so it's probably for the best. Did you decide what you were going to do with Katelyn's dogs?"

"I'm going to keep them," he exclaimed, his smile lifting again. "I must say, I've grown quite fond of them. I thought they would be nuisances, but I understand why Katelyn adored them so much.

They're such little characters. I've got too used to their nails scratching on the floorboards to not have them around now. It might be nice to have some company."

"Until the *right* woman comes along."

"Have you ever tried online dating?" he asked curiously, a brow arching. "I hear it's all the rage these days. Swiping left and right, not that I understand it. Maybe I'll give it a go and see who is out there?"

"Why not?" Liz said before pulling Christopher into a hug. "Think about it a little longer before you propose next time."

"Deal."

Christopher went to leave the shop but stopped in his tracks. He pulled a sheet of paper from his inside pocket as he turned around, a curious look on his face.

"I almost forgot," he said as he unfolded the paper. "I don't suppose it matters very much, but I checked those online ancestry records. Based on what you told me about your family, I managed to go quite far back. Look who I found."

Christopher handed over a black and white family tree, which started with Liz at the bottom and branched up to dozens of names. One of the names three rows above hers had been circled multiple times in red pen.

"*Murphy Jones*?" Liz whispered as she squinted at the information written underneath it. "Born 1884 and died in 1963. Is this –"

"The famous artist," Christopher said with a pleased smile. "He's your great-great-uncle on your father's side. It turns out you have serious talent running through those fingers of yours."

Liz tried to hand the paper back to Christopher, but he insisted she keep it. When he left the shop, she stared at the circled name for minutes before chuckling and tucking it away in her pocket.

"Murphy Jones," Liz whispered as she locked up the shop. "I'm related to *the* Murphy Jones."

After grabbing the biggest bouquet of flowers that the corner shop sold, she set off to the farm to thank them for letting her stay. She was greeted by Sandra, who adored the blooms and claimed not to remember the last time she had been bought flowers, even though John insisted it had only been on her birthday four months ago. When they told her Simon was in the sitting room, she walked through on her own, stopping in her tracks when she saw Nancy by the fire.

"Hello, stranger," Nancy said uncertainly. "How's the murderer hunting going?"

"*Retired*," Liz said with a chuckle as she walked cautiously into the sitting room. "Oh, I've missed you, Nancy."

"I've missed you too!" Nancy cried, jumping up and throwing her arms around Liz as she had on the first day they had met. "Being mad at you was eating away at me. I get it. Who would have thought Debbie Downer would be behind that whole thing? And the body in the chest? They're saying she did that *months* ago, and he's been sitting there. I don't even want to think about it."

"Images like that stay with you," Simon said as he stared blankly into the fire. "Forever, I imagine."

"I should go," Nancy said, already standing up. "I wanted to stop by to share my good news."

"Good news?" Liz echoed. "What's happened?"

Nancy looped her hand around Liz's before leading her out of the sitting room, through the kitchen, and into the tiny stone vestibule. She flicked on the exposed light bulb above them before picking up a canvas that was leaning against the wall; Liz had walked right by it not noticing it.

"'*Lovers Lost*' found again," Nancy said as she turned the painting of Lewis around, the tear no longer there. "I found this at the gallery this morning in the storeroom. It seems Catherine wasn't all bad. She did quite a good job on the repair, don't you think?"

Liz ran her finger along the seam, which now looked like nothing more than a faint scar on the canvas. It took all her energy not to well up.

"It's perfect," she said, her fingers wrapping around the frame. "Thank you for finding this."

"*Ah, ah, ah*!" Nancy said, pulling the canvas away. "You can't have it back. Not quite yet, at least. But you'll still be able to see it."

"What do you mean?"

"I'm putting it on display," Nancy said through a badly concealed grin. "You're looking at the new manager of the gallery! The owner rang me this morning. Apparently, they want to go in a younger and fresher direction after their last two managers were murdered."

"That's amazing!" Liz exclaimed. "Well, not about the murders, but about the promotion! I'm so proud of you."

"And they're doubling my salary," she said with a girlish squeak. "My first act as manager is to get rid of those stuffy paintings that no one has wanted to see for the last century, and replace them with newer, more modern *local* art."

"They couldn't have picked a better person for the job."

"I know," Nancy said with a wink. "I'm going to rule that place *fairly*, and if the power ever gets to my head, you have permission to slap me. Promise not to go too far and put me on display because between you and me, I'm a tiny bit worried that the job title might be a little cursed."

"You and curses!" Liz chuckled. "You have nothing to worry about. The curse has been lifted, and Debbie is well and truly behind bars. And I promise, not only to keep you in check but to be a better friend. Detective Liz might have taken over, and pushed Scarlet Cove Liz out of the way for a little bit."

After one last hug, Nancy left with the painting, leaving Liz to walk back into the kitchen where Simon was waiting for her. She melted into his side, glad to be back to normal again with nothing more than her shop, her painting, and her boyfriend on the horizon.

"I'll miss having you around every day," Simon said as they watched the sunset through the kitchen window.

"Let's say it was a trial."

"How did it go?"

"Well, I don't want to cancel my membership yet," Liz said, resting her hand on Simon's chest. "Who knows? I may even buy the full subscription one day."

"The subscription comes with two conditions."

"Oh?"

"Condition one," Simon started. "No more investigating."

"Deal," Liz said, her fingers crossed behind his back. "And the second?"

"Don't ever try to bake cookies again," he said. "Please."

Liz uncrossed her fingers; that was a promise she could keep.

"Deal."

"Perfect," Simon said, resting his head on hers as the orangey sun bled into an inky horizon. "And maybe next time I ask the first question, you won't cross your fingers behind my back."

"I don't know what you're talking about."

"Sure," he whispered before kissing her on the head. "Why don't we continue the trial for one night, but this time in my cottage?"

"The neighbours will talk," she replied with a playful grin. "It will be quite the local scandal."

"Let them talk," Simon said before cupping her face to kiss her passionately. "But first, the chickens need feeding."

"Lead the way, farm boy!"

Liz followed Simon out of the farmhouse towards the chicken enclosure. She watched from the side as he scattered feed into the flock of birds. Looking back at the small town on the coast as the last of the sun triggered the streetlamps, she thought about how she could get quite used to this life.

Now that you're finished, don't forget to review on **AMAZON** and **GOODREADS**!

If you enjoyed *Dead in the Water*, why not sign up to Agatha Frost and Evelyn Amber's **free** newsletters at **AgathaFrost.com** and **EvelynAmber.com** to hear about brand new releases!

A new Scarlet Cove book will be coming later in the year!

Made in the USA
Monee, IL
23 July 2020

36926871R00173